"I don't want this,"

Summer said breathlessly.

"I don't suppose it matters much whether you want it to happen or not," Chase said, looking down at her with no smile at all on his face. "Sooner or later we'll be lovers, Summer."

"I'm not one of your easy-come, easy-go women." She felt each throb of her heart as passion and panic combined to thicken her blood.

"No, you sure aren't, are you? You're no more what I ought to want than I'm what you should want, but the only way you can keep me from having you, Summer, is to fire me—now. Are you going to do that?"

She looked at him and said nothing.

"I didn't think so," he said softly. "I'll give you a little time, boss lady, to get used to the idea. But not much."

MARRY ME, Cowboy

COWBOYS DO IT BEST

Eileen Wilks

Kids & Kin

Silhouette® Books

Published by Silhouette Books

America's Publisher of Contemporary Romance

SILHOUETTE BOOKS

ISBN 0-373-65341-7

COWBOYS DO IT BEST

Copyright © 1997 by Eileen Wilks

This edition published by arrangement with Harlequin Books S.A.

® and TM are trademarks of Harlequin Books S.A., used under license.
Trademarks indicated with ® are registered in the United States Patent
and Trademark Office, the Canadian Trade Marks Office and in other
countries.

Visit Silhouette Books at www.eHarlequin.com

Printed in U.S.A.

EILEEN WILKS

is a fifth-generation Texan. Her great-great-grandmother came to Texas in a covered wagon shortly after the end of the Civil War—excuse us, the War Between the States. But she's not a full-blooded Texan. Right after another war, her Texan father fell for a Yankee woman. This obviously mismatched pair proceeded to travel to nine cities in three countries in the first twenty years of their marriage, raising two kids and innumerable dogs and cats along the way. For the next twenty years they stayed put, back home in Texas again—and still together.

Eileen figures her professional career matches her nomadic upbringing, since she's tried everything from drafting to a brief stint as a ranch hand—raising two children and any number of cats and dogs along the way. Not until she started writing did she "stay put," because that's when she knew she'd come home. Readers can write to her at P.O. Box 4612, Midland, TX 79704-4612.

Please address questions and book requests to:
Silhouette Reader Service
U.S.: 3010 Walden Ave., P.O. Box 1325, Buffalo, NY 14269
Canadian: P.O. Box 609, Fort Erie, Ont. L2A 5X3

This book is for my daughter Katie, whose "horse sense" was as necessary to my story as her patience with her distracted mother has been to my writing. Thanks, Katie.

One

Three days after leaving Birds' Eye, Wyoming, Chase McGuire killed his truck. It died when he was twenty miles outside of San Antonio, and still 277 miles from his new job on an offshore drilling rig.

Built like the rodeo champion he'd been until last year, and dressed like the cowboy he still was, Chase had a lived-in sort of face that looked a bit older than its thirty-two years. His collection of smile lines said he was accustomed to the tricks life got up to from time to time, and generally took them in stride.

He wasn't smiling now.

Chase stood with the hood up on his three-year-old pickup truck and stared at his engine, so blasted disgusted with himself he could hardly see straight. The air stank of hot metal and burned oil. Chase didn't need the smell, though, or the sight of his oil-free dipstick to tell him he'd messed up royally this time. When the gentle tap-tap-tap that had worried him for the last few miles suddenly mutated into a loud clang-clang-clang just before he coasted off onto the shoulder, he'd known all too well what was wrong.

It was a clear case of negligent homicide. His dash instruments had gone out about fifty miles back. A fuse, he'd thought, and hadn't stopped. He was due in Port Arthur that evening and still had a lot of miles to cover. Maybe he should have gotten an earlier start this morning, but Fannie had been mighty persuasive about lingering. What kind of gentleman would turn down a request from the lady who'd been kind enough to put a weary traveler up for the night?

Especially when his hostess was built the way Fannie was.

He hadn't figured he'd have any trouble making the time up. Of course, he hadn't counted on some unknown road hazard puncturing his radiator during the fifty miles after his instrument panel went dark. He'd lost all his water and coolant and burned up his fuel pump, followed pretty damn fast by his motor.

Chase slammed the hood closed and walked back to the cab. He climbed up, grabbed his keys and the duffel bag that sat on the seat. He started to get out, but the sun catcher that hung from his rearview mirror caught his eye.

A friend had given him the little stained glass rainbow years ago, back when Chase left college to go on the pro rodeo circuit full-time. She'd told him he was chasing rainbows.

Chase hadn't argued. Sure, rainbows were mostly illusion—a trick of light and moisture that fooled you into thinking you saw a bit of magic. But a man needed a rainbow or two to follow. He'd hung that sun catcher on his rearview mirror and followed it through thirty states, mailing his trophies and buckles back to his brother to keep for him.

Until last year. Fifteen months ago, to be exact.

Chase slipped the rainbow's chain free from the mirror. He stuck it in the pocket on the duffel, stepped down from the cab and looked up and down the quiet country road.

Back the way he'd come lay the interstate. Chase preferred a more wandering sort of road, a road with more personality, some surprises along the way.

No, he couldn't think of any reason to backtrack. The way he'd been headed, now, there were a dozen little towns spotting the countryside around San Antonio, clustered up as close and friendly as freckles on a redhead. Most of those tiny towns had a split identity these days, divided between their rural upbringing and their newer function as bedroom communities for the growing city at their center. There was bound to be one of those freckle-sized towns up the road a ways. He'd just walk until he came to it, or until someone took pity on his feet and gave him a lift.

Not that he had any idea in hell what he'd do when he got wherever he was going. He probably had enough cash on him for a tune-up. Not a new engine.

Chase put his good hat on his head and left the old one locked up in the truck, slung his tote over his shoulder and set off down the two-lane road.

He limped. He ignored that, just like he'd been doing for the past fifteen months.

The air was crisp, but hardly January cold. San Antonio was pretty far south, so far that the grass was still green. Good walking weather, he told himself.

Yeah, this was one of life's better jokes, all right, he

thought as his feet put a low hill between him and his pickup. A real zinger. Not that he was crazy about working on an oil rig in the Gulf of Mexico. He'd done enough roughnecking from time to time, filling in between rodeos when he was starting out, to know what the work was like. But he needed something. A goal. Some kind of direction to aim at. He didn't know exactly what he needed, but he sure as hell had to find out.

Chase had always played hard. Before he started shaving he'd understood that the only way to deal with life was to enjoy every moment you can and not take anything too seriously, because sure as anything, once you let something or someone matter too much, life pulled the rug out from under you. But ever since he'd left the circuit, he'd been playing too hard. Drinking too much and working too little. He'd started a slide down a smooth, steep shaft that led exactly nowhere.

When he woke up one morning with chunks of the night before missing, as well as most of the paycheck from his current two-bit job, he'd scared himself badly enough to take the job a friend of a friend offered him in Port Arthur.

Only now he wasn't going to make it to Port Arthur.

Chase's mouth drew into an unaccustomedly grim line. He'd just have to get himself straightened out some other way. He settled his tote on his other shoulder to get the weight off the side with the bad knee.

It took Chase less than a mile to decide that the road just didn't look the same when you were hoofing it in cowboy boots with a bum knee.

Things could be worse, he told himself as he paused to stand, hip shot and thumb out, on the side of the highway as a big semi rumbled toward him. He could've broken down along one of those hundred-miles-of-nothing stretches back in Wyoming with freezing temperatures and snow for company. Around here, though, it wouldn't be long before someone…

The semi thundered past in a rush of hot wind. Chase sighed, tugged down his hat and started walking again.

Not much traffic along this highway at one-fifteen in the afternoon.

Five minutes later, when the woman in the battered blue pickup slowed and pulled over, Chase knew his luck had finally taken a turn for the better. The woman who leaned out the window had thick arms, left bare in spite of the chilly air, with a rose tattoo on the left forearm.

She was the best thing Chase had seen all day.

As soon as the truck stopped, Chase started toward it at something like a trot in spite of his knee. A grin broke out across his face. "Hey, Rosie!" he yelled. "Have you finally decided to get rid of your old man and give me a try?"

The truck door opened, and a big woman leaned out. Her long ponytail was as red as Lady Clairol could make it, and the smile on her face puffed her cheeks out into twin moons. Her voice was as clear and pure as a church bell. "Chase McGuire, you idiot, what are you doing in Texas? Haven't we passed a law against you or something? Come on, get in the truck, you fool."

"That's my Rosie," Chase said, grinning like the fool she'd called him. He slung his tote in the back and climbed into the truck driven by the wife of an old rodeo buddy. "I can't believe it. What are you doing around here? I thought you and Will had settled up in Oklahoma after he retired."

"His ma isn't doing so well. We packed up Joe— he's the only one of the kids still at home—and came down to live with her last fall," Rosie said, putting the gearshift through its paces with all the ease of a professional truck driver—which she had been, years ago. "She runs a couple hundred head just north of here and lives in Bita Creek. That's Bita Creek you see dead ahead," she added.

They were headed downhill at a steady seventy miles an hour toward a scattering of houses and buildings and trees—one of those freckle-sized towns Chase had counted on being nearby. He sorted through his recollections of Will Stafford, a man who'd been one of the best rodeo clowns in the business until stiffening joints and slowed reflexes made him retire. "I thought Will didn't get along with his mom."

"He don't. And the old bat still hates my guts, too," Rosie said cheerfully, slowing as they encountered the bar and gas station that signaled the outskirts of Bita Creek. "But what are you gonna do? She's family."

Chase nodded. He knew what she meant. If your family needed help, you helped. That's all there was to it. Chase, of course, didn't really need help. He was in a temporary bind, that was all. He could straighten this out just fine on his own, without calling Mike. Chase knew exactly how his big brother would react if he knew about Chase's money problems.

No, Chase definitely wasn't going to call on his family for help right now.

"You could'a knocked me down with a feather when I saw you strolling along the side of the road. What's up? That your truck I saw broke down a couple miles back?"

Chase gave her a quick rundown of his recent past.

He was good at making a story out of the banana peels life slipped under his feet, and Rosie laughed until she was wiping tears from her eyes. "Lordy," she said, "you are one unlucky bastard, aren't you? But don't worry. Will knows lots of folks hereabouts, and anyone he don't know, his ma does. He'll find you some sort of job." She reached over and patted his knee reassuringly.

Chase managed not to wince. Not that Rosie was the least bit rough. In spite of her manner and her build, she had gentle, almost dainty hands, as any number of wounded animals and banged-up kids over the years could testify. But even a normal pat hurt his knee right now, sore and swollen as it was from all his walking. That wasn't Rosie's fault. Somehow in telling Rosie about himself, Chase had neglected to mention the horse that had halfway crippled him last year.

"You know me, Rosie," he said, with something close to his usual grin. "I never worry."

Summer Callaway stood in the slanting light of the early morning sun in her bedroom. Twenty hours ago, the Bates's sorrel gelding had tossed her on her left shoulder in the training pen, busting her collarbone and her budget, and plumb ruining her temper.

Summer considered herself a patient woman. She wasn't a whiner, either. She just didn't deal well with frustration.

Getting dressed wasn't easy with a cracked collarbone and a dislocated shoulder, but so far she'd managed to pull on her panties, jeans and socks. It had hurt, but so did walking. Or sitting. Or breathing. She could live with that. Her hair—well, she'd gotten Maud to wash it for her last night after the pain pills kicked in, so at least it was clean. But she couldn't pin it up or braid it or do anything to get it out of her way. It hung halfway down her back, some of the strands catching on the blasted clavicle brace Dr. O'Connor had strapped her into at the emergency room yesterday. That brace was supposed to keep her stable so she didn't jostle her collarbone, but as far as she could tell, all it was good for was making it hell to take a shower. But she was mostly clean now and nearly dressed, and she figured Ricky could help her get her boots on before he went to school.

That left her with one little problem. Her bra.

Who'd have thought a woman who regularly mastered fifteen hundred pounds of some of the orneriest creatures God put on this earth would be defeated by a brassiere?

There was just no damned way to fasten the thing one-handed. She'd thought she could fasten it in front, then turn it around and ease her arms through the straps—but whichever end she wasn't holding fell down.

She chewed on her lip, then stepped over to the worn, maple dresser that had been her mother's once upon a time. By bending her knees to lower herself a bit, she managed to pin the bra between the dresser and her waist. But she couldn't make the hooks come together by wishing, and one hand just wasn't going to get the job done. "Damn!"

"That's another quarter, Mom!" called her son's voice.

"Right," she muttered, standing straight and letting the stupid bra fall to the floor. Summer *never* went braless. Not only was it impractical for a 36-C woman who rode horses to forgo support, she didn't... well, she just didn't.

Today, though, it looked like she would.

"That's seventy-five cents you owe the penalty box so far this morning," Ricky said from the bathroom. She heard the water come on. The rest of her son's words were distorted by the toothbrush he tried to talk around. "And a buck seventy-five from yesterday."

"Yesterday didn't count," Summer said automatically. She began the laborious process of getting her left arm into the sleeve of a flannel shirt, holding her wrist in her good hand and guiding it through the armhole. "Maud agreed. Those pain pills had me temporarily incapacitated." *Ow, ow, ow and damn.* Summer managed to keep the curse silent this time.

She heard Ricky enthusiastically spitting out the toothpaste. Spitting was the one part of toothbrushing he liked. "Yeah, but you said fifty cents' worth before Aunt Maud got you to take the pain stuff."

Strictly speaking, she'd said a good deal more than that, but Ricky hadn't been around to hear it. She'd injured herself while he was at school. His "Aunt Maud"—a friend and neighbor, actually, rather than a blood relation—had driven Summer to the emergency room and waited with her. Maud had called the parents of the students Summer was supposed to teach riding to that day, too. She felt mortified just thinking about it. A riding teacher didn't build confidence in the students or their parents by falling off her horse.

Maud had insisted on hanging around after bringing Summer home, fixing supper and nagging until bedtime. Summer hadn't protested very hard. Not only had she been hurting like hellfire, there wasn't much point.

People mostly did do what Maud Hoppy told them to do. Even Summer.

Buttoning the shirt one-handed wasn't so bad. It only took her twice as long as usual.

"I tell you what, champ," Summer said when she heard the water in the bathroom cut off. She blinked rapidly to make her eyes stop watering and reached for the pale blue sling they'd given her yesterday. "I'll pay up for yesterday if you can tell me what I owe, counting today. That's fifty cents plus seventy-five cents."

Silence. Math wasn't one of her seven-year-old son's strong points. Ricky took an avid interest in money, though, which was one of the reasons for the penalty box they both contributed to for minor infractions. Summer was confident she'd end up paying that box for her bad language yesterday and today. There was a new superhero movie showing in town, and the penalty box didn't have quite enough in it yet to cover their tickets.

Settling her arm in the sling helped. She took a deep breath before opening the door, feeling more unsteady than she wanted to admit. She'd already taken ibupro-fin, and she was determined not to fuzz up her head with a pain pill during the day. She'd get by. She was good at that, wasn't she?

All the rooms in her little two-bedroom house were practically on top of each other, so she saw right away that the bathroom was empty. It was surprisingly tidy, though. Ricky's pajamas weren't in their usual morning spot on the floor. She glanced down the hall.

The bedroom at the end of the hall was Ricky's. She saw right away that he had drawn his bedspread up over his pillow in his best effort at bed making. Action heroes climbed, crawled, leaped and mutated all over the twin bed.

That's love, she thought, a lump in her throat. *That's real love.* He'd already helped out by getting up early and going over to the kennel with her to feed their canine boarders. But bed making was about the most useless activity Ricky could imagine, something mothers insisted on for mysterious feminine reasons no seven-year-old boy could hope to understand. He'd made his up bed simply because it was important to *her.*

How had she ever gotten so lucky? Lord knew Ricky hadn't drawn the best parent material. She did her best, but she didn't know much about being a mother, having been raised without one herself. She'd been winging it since the day he was born. As for his father...whatever Jimmie's sins had been, Summer reminded herself as she started down the short hall towards the kitchen, he'd paid for them. Paid dearly.

"You hungry this morning, champ?" she asked dryly as she entered the kitchen. Ricky was already at the table piling cereal into his mouth with that dribbly, rapid-action motion of his, greedy as any baby bird. The part in his dark hair was crooked, but he'd remembered to put on clean jeans as well as a clean shirt. The crumbs scattered around the cereal bowl told her he'd had one or more of the leftover muffins and hadn't bothered with a plate. As usual.

She skipped the plate lecture and went to the cupboard for a coffee mug. When she reached up, though, even with her good arm, the motion pulled on the muscles attached to her collarbone.

Damn damn damn damn...

"Mom? You okay?"

"Sure," she managed to say, and got the mug. "Did you feed Amos?" Since the huge orange tabby was sitting in her chair, daring her smugly to move him, she figured Ricky had already taken care of the cat. She just wanted to get his attention away from her for a minute, until she got her breath back.

How was she going to get through half the things that had to be done that day? Some of it she flat couldn't do, like cleaning the kennels. She'd have to hire someone. Only there was no way she could afford it. The electric bill was due. Her quarterly tax payment was coming up. Then there were the property taxes, which had doubled this year. They were past due.

About the only thing paid up-to-date was the note she'd been forced to take out on the land when she inherited a rundown stable operation and a pile of medical bills after her father died. Summer paid that bill religiously. Maybe her priorities had been screwed up when she was eighteen, but not anymore. Nothing could be allowed to endanger her land.

"One twenty-five," Ricky announced suddenly. "You owe the box a buck twenty-five, Mom."

"I guess you got me." She ruffled his hair with her good hand, making him duck and grimace, as she brought her coffee over to the table.

Fifteen minutes later Ricky tore out the back door, his backpack slung over one shoulder, making his usual mad dash for the school bus stop down the road. She glanced at the clock and sipped her second cup of coffee. Seven-thirty. Normally she'd start cleaning the dog pens about now. Today...well, she didn't think she could shovel poop one-armed, but maybe she should try. Fortunately, the kennel only held five dogs right now. January was slow.

Well, she thought, pushing away from the table, sitting here brooding didn't accomplish much. She'd do what she could and let the rest go, then come back to the house and find some way to squeeze enough from her budget to hire someone.

Summer grabbed the keys to the kennel from their hook by the door, stepped out onto the wooden porch at the back of her house, and got assaulted. Kelpie knew better than to jump up, so she ran in tight little circles and yipped. The black-and-white Border collie mix was supposed to be Ricky's dog, but she adored everyone impartially. Two years ago Summer had found Kelpie huddled outside her fence, obviously abandoned. The dog had needed food, love and 132 dollars' worth of trips to the vet to regain her health, and she'd been rejoicing ever since. Summer smiled and managed to stroke Kelpie's head a few times before the animal raced off in delight.

At the end of the porch, Hannah, the aging bloodhound who had belonged to Summer's father, limited her greeting to a dignified thump-thump of her tail.

A breath of wind stirred the sign at the main gate, the one that read "Three Oaks Kennel and Stable" with the little drawing of the oak tree on it. Summer inhaled deeply, enjoying the slight bite in the air, even enjoying the smell of the nearby stable—a smell that meant horses and home.

Some people liked to wander, she knew. Not her, not anymore. Running off with Jimmie had taught her that much. Summer needed roots. She needed to be on her own land, in her own house, with the people who were important to her nearby.

She was a lucky woman, Summer thought as she started across the big, grassy yard, heading for the kennel. She was living the life she wanted, she had a bright, wonderful son she loved more than her next heartbeat, and she'd learned a valuable lesson while still young.

Men were too damned much trouble. Period.

She had just reached the paddock that lay between the house and the kennel when a huge old Buick pulled up next to the chain-link fence that surrounded the front part of her property. Summer slowed and shook her head. She knew that car.

The woman who got out was as tiny as her car was big. She was a dried-up little dab of a woman in a faded cotton dress, with a face like crumpled tissue and thin white hair scraped back in a bun. "Summer!" the little old lady bellowed. "What do you think you're doing? Didn't I tell you I'd come over and take care of those dogs this morning?"

All bones and mouth, that was Maud Hoppy. Summer stopped. "Yes, you did. And I told you not to."

Maud slammed the door of her tank shut and walked over to the small gate, the people-sized one just west of the big, truck-sized gate. "Don't know what difference you thought that would make."

Exasperated, Summer propped her good hand on her hip. "You're nearly eighty, Maud. You don't need to be shoveling dog poop."

"I'm seventy-one." Maud always lied very positively. She closed the gate behind her. "And I'm not going to shovel poop. I'll just feed the silly things. Do you need me to feed the horses, too?"

"Ricky and I already fed the dogs. As for the horses, I got hold of Raul last night. He's already been and gone." Raul usually worked in the afternoons during the week, but he'd agreed to come early that morning to take care of the stable chores before school. He wouldn't do the kennel, though. The strapping sixteen-year-old hunk of Latin machismo was afraid of dogs. Not that he'd ever admit it, of course.

"Good, then you and I can go back inside and drink coffee while you figure out how much you can afford to pay a hand for the next two months." Maud took Summer's good elbow and pulled. Her snowy white head barely reached Summer's shoulder.

"Two months is impossible," Summer said, towed reluctantly back towards the house by her tiny friend.

"The doctor said two months."

"Dr. O'Connor doesn't have to pay my bills," she retorted. "I have to pay his."

Still, somehow Summer found herself seated at her kitchen table with her checkbook, a pad and paper, and a computer printout of her current bills and projected expenses in front of her. Her shoulder throbbed in rhythm with her pulse as she added up a column of figures while Maud darted around the kitchen like a hummingbird, looking for things to clean.

Summer hoped Maud found something to clean soon. If she didn't, she was apt to start cooking, and Summer really couldn't afford to throw out whatever mess resulted. "Sit down and drink some coffee."

"In a minute." Maud pounced on the toaster, unplugging it and taking it over to the sink to shake the crumbs out. "Have you figured out how much you can afford to pay?"

"Yeah." Nothing. That's what she could afford. But by making a partial payment on her property taxes and putting the rest off another month or two—they weren't going to seize her land, she assured herself, even if she was late—she could pay everything else that was due and hire someone for a while. "It's not going to be easy finding someone, though. Getting someone who knows horses and doesn't mind that the job is temporary—''

"Now there," Maud announced in her raspy, Mae West voice, "I can help." She turned around, toaster in hand, polishing it as she spoke. "You know Will Stafford?"

"You know I do, Maud. His wife Rosie and I are on the SPCA board together in Bica. But their son Joe already has a part-time job, doesn't he?"

"I'm not talking about Joey. Last night Will was calling around, trying to find someone who needs a hand. Seems Will is helping out an old buddy from his rodeo days—"

"A rodeo bum." Summer's lip curled.

"Now, don't you be judging everyone by that husband of yours. And it doesn't matter, anyway, whether this fellow is like your Jimmie was or not. He's desperate. Seems his truck died and he's about broke. You could board him in that little room off the kennel and pay him real cheap."

Maud sounded so satisfied with the poor man's plight that Summer couldn't help grinning. "Still, if the man is anything like Jimmie, I'd have a battle getting my money's worth, no matter how little I paid him."

"Jimmie was lazy. This fellow, though—I don't imagine a fellow gets to be 'Best All-Around Cowboy' at the NFR without working for it. Besides, Will Stafford vouches for him."

Summer frowned. "So who is this paragon?"

"Chase McGuire."

"Chase McGuire?" she asked disbelievingly.

Maud put the toaster back where it belonged. "I'll

just make us some more coffee,'' she announced. ''You know this McGuire?''

Summer stood up. ''Not really. I'll make the coffee, Maud. I'm not helpless.'' At least the coffee would be drinkable if Summer made it. She managed to beat Maud to the coffeepot, grabbed the glass carafe and took it to the sink.

She and Jimmie hadn't exactly run in the same crowd as Chase McGuire. Jimmie had never made it near the top, while the other man had stayed high in the rankings for years. Why would such a man be interested in a two-bit job?

While the carafe filled with water, Summer used her good hand to shift her left arm in the sling, trying to ease the ache. ''I've never actually met him, Maud. But no one who's been involved with rodeo could help knowing who he is. I saw him around sometimes, back when I made the circuit with Jimmie.'' Oh, yes, she'd seen him. She remembered his lean build, his shaggy blond hair and that deadly smile. And the women. She remembered that, too. He'd attracted women the way horses draw flies. ''A man like that would never be satisfied with this sort of penny-ante job,'' she said, and shut off the water. ''No, he wouldn't work out.''

''He'll be here in thirty minutes.''

Summer gaped at her friend. ''He...he—''

''Will's at work, so I told Rosie to bring him by to talk to you about the job at nine-thirty. That seemed like plenty of time.''

How was it she'd never noticed that sly gleam in her friend's faded blue eyes before? ''I do not want Chase McGuire coming here. I won't hire him, so it's just a waste of my time and his. You'll have to call Rosie back, Maud. I'm not changing my mind on this.''

"We've just got time to dust the living room before they get here,'' Maud said.

Two

Thirty-two minutes later, Chase McGuire stood at her door, hat in hand, with Rosie Stafford. Rosie wore an orange blouse that went with her fiery hair about the same way that Tabasco sauce goes with jalapeños. Chase McGuire wore jeans, a sky blue shirt and that dangerous smile of his. He was a tall man, with just enough creases in his face to make it interesting. He had dark eyelashes, and his hair was six shades of blond all stirred up together.

Summer looked at the man standing at her front door and realized she'd been fooling herself when she thought she knew anything about him. Seeing Chase McGuire at a distance, hearing the gossip about him, was totally different from meeting him up close and personal. He radiated bad-boy charm the way a stove gives off heat.

Summer managed not to stutter when she told the

two of them to come on in. "Have a seat, Rosie," she
said, gesturing at the old plaid sofa that Maud had vac-
uumed free of cat hair less than ten minutes before.
"And...Mr. McGuire, too, of course."

"Make that Chase," he said, treating her to a smile
that showed off the single dimple in his left cheek.
"Otherwise I might forget to answer. 'Mr. McGuire' is
my big brother, Mike."

"Of course." No, she'd never known this man. He
made her feel...*stupid,* she thought. *Stupid* was definitely the word for what she was feeling. "Sit down,
Chase. Can I get you something? Some coffee?"

Summer noticed two things when Chase followed
Rosie to the couch. First, he limped. Not badly, but the
stiffness in his stride was especially noticeable in a man
so surely made for strength and grace. She also noticed
his...physique. At the mature age of twenty-seven,
Summer was used to considering herself past the age
for youthful follies. She was dismayed to learn she
hadn't gotten over her weakness for a cowboy in a
tight-fitting pair of jeans, after all.

"The coffee's fresh," Maud informed them. She was
perched primly on a ladder-back chair, imitating a
proper old lady.

"None for me, thanks," Rosie said, settling herself
into the cushions on the couch with a little grunt.
"Seems like the bigger the rest of me gets, the tinier
my bladder shrinks. Can't drink more'n a couple of
cups these days."

Summer caught the quick glance Chase McGuire
gave her sling before he answered easily, "I don't need
a thing." He sat on the couch. The Stetson he turned
to lay, brim up, on the end table was black with a rolled
brim and a gorgeous band of silver conchas.

Not a hat to wear when mucking out a stall. "I'm not sure what to say," Summer began, seating herself in the old recliner. Leaning against the recliner's high back eased some of the ache in her collarbone and shoulder. "Maud talked to Will without discussing this with me first. I don't know if you realize what the job would be."

"Not exactly," he said. "But I know it involves horses, so I don't figure there's too much of a problem." That grin flashed again. "I'm good with horses."

Yes, the NFR's "Best All-Around Cowboy" a few years back ought to be good with horses. She wondered how he'd managed to go through all his prize money—a small fortune, really—so quickly. Gambling? Women? Not that this man would ever have to pay for a woman, but a lot of cowboys liked to spend whatever money they had on whoever had their attention at the moment.

"I'm sure you can handle horses just fine," she said, "but I need someone to do the dirty work, not the fun stuff. Muck out the stalls, feed the horses, worm them, move them to pasture and back—oh, and probably tack up for me on Mondays and Fridays. I give lessons."

"Now, Summer," Rosie said, "Chase ain't a Hollywood cowboy. He don't mind getting dirty or shoveling out a stall. He'd make you a good hand."

Chase shot his friend an exasperated look. "I'd just as soon apply for the job myself, Rosie."

Summer shifted, trying to find a position that made the hurt go away. "But there are the dogs, too. At the kennel. You'd have to clean up after them, feed them, hose down the runs—and a lot of the owners want their animals bathed before they pick them up. I can't imagine that someone like you would—"

"Ma'am," he interrupted. "I don't know what you mean by 'someone like me,' but what I am is broke. So's my truck, unfortunately. Your job's got two things going for it. One, Rosie tells me you've got a room I might be able to stay in. Two, it's temporary. That suits me, because I don't plan on being here longer than it takes to save up enough to get my truck fixed."

No, Chase McGuire wasn't the type to hang around. "I can't afford to pay much." She couldn't help noticing his eyes. They weren't a plain old brown. Like amber glass held up to the light so the sunshine streams through, they seemed lit from within. Like he had something burning inside him.

"How much is not much?"

Summer didn't like the way he was looking at her, all warm and approving—as if he'd noticed her noticing his eyes. She said stiffly, "Two hundred a week, with the room Rosie mentioned and two meals a day thrown in. I'd need you on Saturday and Sunday, too, at least at first."

"Well," he said, his smile widening, "if that's an offer, you've got me, honey, for as long as you need me."

She frowned. "I didn't—"

"Good!" Maud boomed as she bounced out of her chair. "Glad we got that settled. You made a smart decision, Summer."

"I didn't—"

"You might as well get your stuff from the truck, Chase," Rosie said, heaving herself to her feet. "I imagine Summer wants to put you to work right away."

"His room's at the kennel," Maud told Rosie. "I'd be glad to show it to him. It isn't much, but the bed's decent and the smell's not bad. There's even a half bath

Summer's daddy built on, when he had a hand working here full-time.''

''I'm sure Chase'll like it just fine, after sleeping on that old couch of mine last night,'' Rosie said. ''Well, Chase, I wouldn't say you've landed in clover exactly. Maybe a big pile of horse dung soft enough to cushion the fall.'' She chuckled. ''And Summer, honey, don't you worry about Chase. He's a rascal, but an honest one. You might have to knock him on the side of the head a time or two, but he'll do you a good job. You'll be glad you hired him.''

I didn't, Summer thought, but Maud picked up where Rosie left off, telling Chase how much he was going to like working at the Three Oaks. Summer couldn't get a word in edgewise.

She glanced at Chase and saw that he was thoroughly aware of her predicament. His eyes were brimful of mirth.

Her lips twitched in spite of herself. ''All right,'' she said. ''All right! The two of you can quit trying to out-talk me and embarrass me into hiring Chase. I do need a hand, and he's willing to work cheap. And,'' she said, sliding him a look, ''like you said, Rosie, I can always knock him on the side of the head if I need to.''

And really, she assured herself, in spite of her un-settling reaction to this man, she didn't have anything to worry about. After Jimmie, she was immune to the superficial appeal of a good-looking traveling man.

''Then I'll just do like I was told,'' Chase said, standing and smiling that easy smile of his, ''and get my bag from the truck. I figured that if you did hire me, you'd need me to get to work right away, so I brought my stuff along. I hope you don't mind…ma'am.''

Somehow, when spoken in his low, molasses-sweet

voice *ma'am* sounded more like *honey* or *sweetheart*. Something restless and unwelcome stirred in her, a sensation as hot and ominous as the rumbling approach of a summer storm. "Of course not," she said, a bit too sharply. "Come on. I'll show you your room and get you started at the kennel." She stood up, turned to say something to Maud…and then stood there, blinking foolishly, disoriented by the fierce grinding pain that seized her.

She'd forgotten her collarbone. She'd moved without taking her disability into account, and jarred the break. How could she have forgotten like that?

A big, warm hand cupped her good elbow, steadying her. "You all right?" Chase's deep voice asked softly.

She turned her head and looked right into amber eyes with the mirth for once completely gone. Concerned eyes, thickly fringed with those dark, ridiculous lashes. She was close enough to see the texture of the skin stretched across his smooth-shaven cheeks. *Men's skin*, she thought fuzzily, *is so different from women's*. Summer looked at Chase's skin and thought of leather, the smooth, supple sort of leather so soft it made you want to pet it, made you want—

"I'm fine," she lied, and pulled her arm away.

Oh, Lord. What had she done?

Fate was a fickle female. Chase had known that before he was old enough to shave. For the first time in fifteen months, though, fate seemed to be favoring him some. He had a job now, with the promise of a roof over his head that wasn't part of an old friend's charity.

Two months wasn't so long, he told himself as he retrieved his bag from Rosie's truck. He could handle being without wheels that long, and he could learn to

— be around horses without having it matter so damned much.

His new employer ought to be a nice distraction. Of course, she hadn't really wanted to hire him. He had the distinct impression Summer Callaway didn't trust him.

Smart woman.

He really ought to leave her alone, he told himself as he headed back to the neat little frame house where the three women were probably picking him apart in his absence. So maybe she did have a body that would make a strong man weak and the prettiest blue eyes he'd seen in a long time. Those blue eyes frosted over every time he smiled at her. He was a rodeo cowboy, after all. Just like Jimmie Callaway had been. Considering what Chase knew about the jerk she'd been married to, he couldn't blame her for wanting to keep her distance.

He frowned at the platoon of tiny toy soldiers and army vehicles blocking the sidewalk up to the house. Summer Callaway was a mother, apparently. He hadn't known that. Not that Chase had anything against mothers. He just didn't get involved with them. Nine times out of ten they were looking for someone to be a daddy to their little ones, and Chase was the world's worst candidate for that role.

"Hey, Rosie," he said, swinging the door open and stepping back into the neat-as-a-pin living room. The house smelled inviting, a friendly mingling of scents: pine cleaner, coffee and vanilla. The room itself was definitely "country," from the maple end tables to the comfortably worn plaid upholstery to the gun rack near the door. Folks who lived in the country tended to take a practical attitude toward guns. They were a necessary tool for dealing with wild dogs, snakes or rabid skunks.

"I hope you haven't been telling all my secrets." He looked from his friend to the slender woman in worn denim, green flannel and a pale blue sling. She stood there watching him with those pretty blue eyes of hers.

Heat. Like a punch in the stomach he felt it again— the same hot, bubbling mix he'd felt when he first laid eyes on her. Anticipation. Hunger. A thrill a lot like the moment when he lowered himself onto the back of an angry bronc in the chute and knew he was in for one hell of a ride.

He smiled.

Rosie chuckled. "I can't tell what I don't know, and I'm sure I don't know all your secrets. Well," she said, and heaved herself to her feet, "I'd better get back to the house. You let me know, Summer, if this rascal gives you any trouble."

Somewhat more reluctantly Maud announced that she had to be going, too. While the three women went through their leave-taking rituals, Chase watched his new boss.

Some might find her a bit on the skinny side, at least from the waist down. Not Chase. The moment she'd opened the door to him, he'd discovered a decided partiality for long, slim legs and a tiny butt, especially when they were matched up with full breasts and hair the color of whiskey in a glass.

He was all but positive she wasn't wearing a bra under that big flannel shirt.

"Well?" she said, facing him as she closed the front door on her friends. "Are you ready to go to work?"

His gaze drifted lazily from her breasts up to her face. He was supposed to leave this woman alone? He shook his head, doubting himself already, and drawled, "I'm ready whenever you are, sugar."

Frost warnings went up in those blue eyes. "We'll go out the back door. Come on."

Her house was small, but immaculate. What little he'd seen so far of her operation made him think it would be just as scrupulously tended, too, and he liked that. Chase wasn't especially tidy with his own things, but he was downright nitpicky when it came to horses, their gear, housing and care.

"There's a phone in the barn and another cordless unit in the kennel, but don't worry about answering if it rings," she said, pausing next to the back door to pick up a cordless phone. "I keep one of the cordless phones with me all the time so I can book appointments." She frowned at the phone in her hand. "Dammit, I can't put this on my belt if I can't fasten a belt."

"I'd be glad to help." He couldn't quite say that without smiling.

She turned the frown on him, then turned away, tucking the phone into her sling next to her arm. "The horses have already been taken care of this morning," she told him, opening the back door and ignoring his offer. "Usually I do it, but Raul came over early today as a favor."

And who, he wondered, was Raul, and just what kind of favors did he do for her? Chase liked the idea of doing "favors" for his new boss. He didn't like the idea that someone else might already be doing for her what he was trying to persuade himself he shouldn't do. "Raul?" he asked. "Is he a…friend of yours?"

She paused, holding the door open and looking at him suspiciously. "Why?"

He gave her his most innocent smile. "Just wondered why you didn't offer him the job."

She continued to frown. "Raul is in the eleventh grade. He can't put in the kind of hours I'll need in the next couple of weeks, but he's a good hand."

Chase nodded blandly as desire tightened down another notch. *It doesn't matter if another man is in the picture or not,* he told himself. Not if he intended to keep his distance.

Was that what he intended? "I guess I'll meet Raul this afternoon, then."

"Right," she muttered, giving him one last, wary look. "Well, come on."

She'd barely set foot on the painted gray floor of the wooden porch when a black-and-white tornado shaped like a dog ran up to her, yipping and twisting itself in tight, excited circles. For the first time, Chase saw what Summer looked like when she wasn't suspicious or hurting. When she smiled and meant it.

His breath caught in his chest.

"Hmm?" she said, stroking the head of the frantically happy dog. "Did you say something?"

"Quite a watchdog you have there," he managed to say. *She was beautiful.* It came as a shock. Not just pretty or sexy or desirable. When Summer smiled with that soft look in her eyes, she was flat-out beautiful. "I imagine she'd be hell on a burglar, running around in circles until the poor fellow got dizzy from watching her."

The light in her eyes changed from tenderness to amusement. "Oh, Kelpie here is pretty useless as a watchdog. She loves everybody. But I'd better take you over and introduce you to Hannah." She walked over to where a large brown lump rested on the edge of the porch. The lump lifted its head and thumped its tail once when Summer lowered herself into a careful squat to pet it. "Hannah knows Rosie, so she didn't mind when you two came up to the door, but we'd better give you a formal introduction now."

Did she seriously think that decrepit old hound was a watchdog? Willing to play along, Chase set his bag down and hunkered down beside her. He caught just a whiff of Summer's scent. Strawberries. It made him smile, because it suited her. "Hi, there, Hannah," he said to the lump. "My name's Chase."

"I had something a bit more basic in mind," Summer said dryly. "Here, give me your hand." She reached out and took it.

Heat lightning. That was all Chase could think of when she took his hand in hers—the hot, unexpected stroke of lightning that can flash unpredictably across a cloudless summer sky. Involuntarily, wanting only to hang on to the sensation a moment longer, his hand closed around hers. Her skin was soft, but her hand wasn't. It was a strong hand, tough and capable.

That, too, stirred him.

He heard the hitch in her breath. But she didn't look at him, didn't acknowledge what arced between them. Instead, after a second she said, as level and calm as if nothing had happened, "Now we let Hannah smell our hands, so that she remembers your scent and mine mixed together."

"Sounds like a good idea to me," he said huskily, and stretched out their joined hands. The hound lifted her nose and sniffed at them. "Your scent and mine, mixed together…"

She jerked her hand away. She wasn't quite fast

enough, though, to rise to her feet without Chase's assistance. He got hold of her good arm and steadied her.

Chase didn't want to see all the color drain out of her face again, the way it had earlier. He'd cracked enough bones himself to know she had to be hurting. She wasn't about to admit it, though, or go rest. Chase understood the need to keep on going when it made more sense to quit, and he was beginning to get the idea that this woman had an oversize helping of pride.

She pulled away. "Mr. McGuire, I'd appreciate it if you'd keep your hands to yourself."

Would she, now? "Well, I can't quite promise to do that, ma'am. Not when you've been hurt and are maybe a bit too stubborn to admit you need a hand now and again. But I'll keep what you said in mind."

"That's not what I meant," she said, "and you know it. A man like you is well aware of—"

"Just a minute," he said. "That's the second time you've said that—'a man like me.' Now, I know we've never met. I'd remember. So you must have heard some gossip…or else you're getting me mixed up with someone else. Like your husband, maybe?"

She looked as startled as if he'd reached out and slapped her. "I didn't—you—did you know Jimmie?"

"I ran into him a couple times. Look, I know some rodeo wives get a bad feel for the rodeo and everyone connected with it, especially if their husbands stay on the circuit as much of the year as Jimmie did."

She just gave him a hard, baffled stare and turned and started across the yard. Chase was left to pick up his bag and follow. Had she reacted that way because she'd been so much in love with the good-looking bum she'd been married to? Or did she already know plenty about Jimmie Callaway and just not want to discuss it?

The kennel was a long, cinder block building on the other side of the paddock, about twenty yards from the stable. It was painted white, with trim the same dark green as the little house they'd just left, and typical of what he'd seen so far. Not fancy, but sturdy and well maintained.

Chase automatically slowed when they reached the pole fencing surrounding the paddock so he could look over the four horses inside. Two of them he marked immediately as the sort of plodders she might put a beginner up on for those lessons she'd mentioned. He wouldn't mind getting a leg over either of the other two, though. "That's a fine-looking dun," he said, referring to a mare with a coat a few shades lighter than Summer's own golden brown hair. "She's mostly quarter horse, isn't she?"

Summer paused and glanced back over her shoulder at him, her blue eyes still chilly. "Mostly. She's unregistered, but her dam had a lot of Thoroughbred in her."

He nodded. The mare had the dainty ears and face of a Thoroughbred and the muscular hocks of a quarter horse. At that moment she perked up those pretty ears and ambled toward them. "I've seen some fine horses with that mix. She's yours?"

The compliment pleased her, but she didn't want to be pleased. Not yet. She turned to greet the horse. "Honey-Do and I have been together a long time. I started training her with my father's help when I was nine. The two of us learned barrel racing together. She's pushing twenty now, so mostly I use her for Western pleasure these days."

"Honeydew?" he asked, trying to figure out the reason for the name. "Like the melon?"

"No." Summer reached out her good hand to the

horse, who had her neck stretched out, obviously confident of getting attention. Summer gave the horse a good, brisk rub up the jawbone and along the cheek strap.

Those lovely, capable hands of hers could do a number of things well, Chase felt certain. He could think of one or two in particular he'd like. He could, but he'd better not. Not if he was going to keep his hands off her.

"She started out plain old Honey when I first got her, for her color. I was nine," she said, and spared him a slight smile, "and not especially original. Pretty soon, though, her name became Honey-Do as in, 'Honey, do this,' or 'Honey, do that.' Because Honey does just about anything you ask of her—don't you, sweetheart?" she finished, her voice dropping into a croon.

Everything about her warmed up around animals. He couldn't help wondering what it would take to get her to heat up for him. "What about the paint with the roan markings?" he asked, setting down his duffel. "Is he yours?"

The raw-boned gelding he referred to was a big, ugly brute, maybe seventeen hands high. The animal looked up just then from pulling bites of hay off the bale set in the center of the paddock. When he saw that another horse was getting attention, he snorted and trotted over, using his weight to push Honey-Do aside and stretching out his own big, Roman nose.

"For my sins, he is," Summer said. "He's a two-year-old, so he's not much on manners yet." She turned sideways so the inquisitive horse couldn't nudge her bad shoulder, then had to push his nose away when he started to lip the sleeve of her shirt. "Some cowboy wannabes out of San Antonio bought him and his mother when he was a colt, then lost interest. They sold the mare easily enough, but the future was looking pretty dim for Horatio here when I heard about him three months ago. I picked him up dirt cheap because they didn't really want to sell to the knackers. I'd planned on training him fast in the basics and selling him, but I guess that's not going to happen now."

"I don't know why you couldn't do just that," Chase said, leaning on the top pole to give the jealous Horatio a good scratch behind the ears. "He's not exactly a pretty face, and he's too big for arena work, but his gait looks smooth. I bet he'd make a fine working horse."

"Timing," she said succinctly. "In order to make any money on him, I need to get him trained before he eats up my profit. All I can give him is the basics. Like you said, he's not pretty enough for the arena, and I don't know how to train him for range roping or cutting, so I couldn't expect to get any great price for him."

Chase thought about that. "You've had him on the *longe* line?"

She nodded. "He's stubborn, but he's bright and not easily spooked. He walks, trots and lopes on the *longe* now, and you're right about his gait. I'd just gotten him used to the bridle and was ready to move on to the saddle when this happened." With a nod of her chin she indicated her sling. "Now he'll forget what he knows before I can start working him again."

"You do much training?"

"Right now it's just Horatio and Maverick. That's the Bates's sorrel gelding—the one that dumped me on my shoulder yesterday. They wanted me to get him over some of his bad habits, so I'm working him as well as boarding him." She stared out over the paddock, a frown pleating her brow.

"I'll train them."

That brought her head around fast—too fast, judging by the way she winced. "I'm not paying you trainer's wages."

She was a suspicious one, wasn't she? He smiled. "You don't have to. I figure I might find training a couple of ornery horses a nice change of pace after mucking out stalls and shoveling dog poop."

Her brows lifted skeptically. "You want to train them—just for fun?"

"Sure." He turned and eased a little closer to her. Close enough to make her just a bit uncomfortable, close enough to see the slight, involuntary flare of her nostrils, as though she were catching his scent. "Of course, I might have some other sort of motives mixed in there, like hoping to make you feel real grateful to me. But you're too bright to fall for something like that, aren't you? So I guess I'll have to settle for what I said. A change of pace. A bit of a challenge."

Beneath the frown that lingered on her face lay a sort of puzzled awareness. Her eyes were just a hint wider. A hint uncertain. "I guess if you worked Horatio, you could take a percentage. When I sell him. That would be fair, wouldn't it?"

"Fair?" He did what he'd been wanting to do all morning, and ran his fingers down one long strand of hair, playing with it. "Doesn't seem like it would be all that fair to you." He rubbed the hair between his fingers, savoring the smooth, silky feel of it.

"Don't." Her voice was steady enough, but her eyes gave her away. He saw anger there. Confusion. Arousal. The confusion excited him as much as the arousal, and he didn't like that. Only innocents were confused by their physical needs, and Chase wasn't a man who looked for trophies outside of the arena. He liked his women easy and experienced. Easy meant no one got hurt, no one got burned when it was time to move on down the road.

But he wanted this woman. He wanted to seduce this woman.

His gaze slipped from her face to her throat, where he could see the rapid flutter of her pulse. Lower, to where her hardened nipple was puckered beneath the soft flannel of her shirt...on one side. On the other side was her sling.

He *really* shouldn't be doing this.

The sound of a motor filtered through his lust-induced haze. Summer heard it, too. Her eyes widened. She stepped back. He let his hand fall. She frowned, looked over his shoulder and frowned harder. "Well, shi—shoot."

It amused him that she'd edited out the cussword almost as much as it pained him to be interrupted. He turned.

A tall man was climbing out of a low-slung foreign car next to the smaller gate. Although the man wore boots and a black cowboy hat with his suit, Chase would be willing to bet he'd never sat on a horse. Even from here Chase could see that his face had the smooth, indoor look of a businessman.

"It never rains but it pours," Summer muttered.

"So who is he?"

"Ray Fletcher."

The minute the smooth-faced Ray Fletcher stepped through the gate, the belly-deep belling of a bloodhound erupted from the back porch of the house. Hannah heaved to her feet and bayed again, and a cacophony of barks, yips, yaps and woofs broke out at the kennel.

"Ray," Summer said in a conversational tone that he barely heard over the din, "has never been introduced to Hannah."

Chase grinned. Apparently Hannah was a little more alert than she looked, and she set the other dogs off. You couldn't beat a dozen yapping dogs as an alarm system.

Ray Fletcher closed the gate and started across the thirty or forty yards from the front gate to the paddock. Chase noticed that Summer didn't take one step toward the man. Fletcher had crossed half the distance before she made some kind of signal to Hannah, at which the old dog heaved a sigh and plopped back down. The rest of the canine clamor was dying down by the time Ray Fletcher reached them.

He was an indoor sort of man, all right, a little soft through the middle and under his smooth-shaven chin. Not bad looking. Not especially good-looking, either. There wasn't much memorable about him, Chase decided, except the expensive clothes he wore…and his eyes.

Ray Fletcher's eyes weren't soft when his gaze flicked over Chase as quickly as a lizard's tongue tasting the air, summing him up and dismissing him. Chase didn't much care for the dismissal, but it did intrigue him. Offhand, he could only think of a few men who'd discounted him that quickly. A couple of them were fools. One was as ruthless and cunning as Chase had ever come across.

"Summer," Fletcher said in a pleasant tenor voice, "as soon as I heard about your accident I came to see if there's any way I could help. I know how proud you are, but perhaps you'd consider a loan.''

"Really? And here I thought you'd probably come out here to see if my getting crippled up meant I'd have to sell you my land.''

He looked pained. "I know you've never acquitted me of having ulterior motives for dating you, though I'd think you'd only have to look in the mirror to realize the truth. But mixing business with pleasure is never a good idea. I should have known better.''

"Well, if you're really concerned, Ray, let me reassure you. This is Chase McGuire. He's going to work for me while I'm unable to take care of things myself, so you see, I really don't have any problems for you to concern yourself with. Chase, this is Ray Fletcher, a land shark from San Antonio.''

"For heaven's sake, Summer,'' Fletcher said, exasperated, then turned his quick brown eyes on Chase. "Mrs. Callaway does like to give me a hard time, Mr. McGuire. I'm a real estate developer, and—'' he smiled and shook his head ruefully "—I made the mistake of trying to persuade Summer to sell her land. Now I'm one of the bad guys, as far as she's concerned.''

"Is that so?'' Chase stuck his thumbs in his belt loops and looked Fletcher up and down, his expression easy and pleasant. "You saying you aren't a bad guy? Sure looks to me like a black hat you're wearing.''

Fletcher couldn't decide if that was supposed to be a joke or not, so he ignored it. "Summer,'' he began, "about that loan. I've got the money to spare, you know that. Just say the word.''

"Now why would you think money was tight for me, unless you knew how much my property taxes had jumped this year? They doubled, Ray. And you know what's odd? It was right after I turned down your offer that the appraiser showed up to reappraise my land. Quite a coincidence, isn't it?''

He frowned. ''You can't seriously think I had anything to do with that.''

''You know how us women are, Ray.'' Her voice turned low and cold. ''We get these notions. I'm getting another one right now. I'm thinking you'd love to make me a loan so that you could somehow get me to default on it. That would simplify things for you, wouldn't it? You and your plans for your fancy housing development?''

''Oh, enough.'' Fletcher made a chopping gesture. ''I put my foot wrong with you months ago, but this is getting ridiculous. You can't blame me for every little thing that goes wrong.'' He started to turn, then paused. ''Look,'' he said, ''I really would like to persuade you of my good intentions. If you're ever ready to give me a chance, just call.''

''I'll give you a chance, Ray. Just withdraw your offer for my land. Formally, in writing. And throw in something about how you won't ever make another offer.''

He blinked before replying, a second too late, ''When you get over your paranoia, call me.'' He turned and walked off.

''That got rid of him,'' Chase said when Ray Fletcher was out of earshot.

''Did you hear him?'' Summer stared at Fletcher's retreating back. ''He offered me a loan. A *loan*,'' she repeated, astounded at the insult. ''I can't believe it. He honestly thinks I turned down his offer to buy my land out of some stupid feminine pique. He thinks he can go right on pretending to be interested in me. Like that would make any difference about whether I'd sell the land or not.''

''How much land do you have?'' Chase didn't think a developer would be interested in the little bit of land that the stable, kennel and house sat on.

''All that,'' she said, gesturing at the large, fenced pasture beyond the house and grounds, ''and down from there to the river. Nearly forty acres, ten of it riverfront. My father fought hard to hold on to it. He had land speculators after him, too, always trying to get him to sell, but he held on. I am not,'' she said, ''going to let some inflated property taxes and a sore shoulder make me lose what he held on to.''

Pride, Chase thought. The woman had more of it than was good for her. She was stiff with it, practically quivering with outrage that Fletcher had thought he could get his hands on her land just because she had five times as much of it as she needed and nowhere near enough money—just because she was broke and hurt and might be thought, by some, to be just a tad vulnerable at the moment.

It was damned appealing. ''Forty acres isn't enough to ranch, but it's more than you need to run a stable, isn't it?''

She looked at him, disgusted. ''I don't imagine you'd understand.'' She turned away. ''Come on. The morning's nearly over and the kennels are still dirty.''

Chase watched her walk away. Her back stayed stiff and straight, but her cute little butt swayed gently from side to side. He appreciated the stiffness almost as much as he did the sway. He watched her move and saw how the morning sun turned to copper when it tangled in her long, unbound hair.

He sighed. He was a weak man. A sadly weak man.

And she was a sexy, prideful woman with an injured shoulder who wanted nothing to do with him. A woman like that didn't know enough about her own body's responses to defend herself against him, and he really ought to leave her alone...even though when he touched her hair her breath got shallow and her nipples got hard. Even though he couldn't keep from speculating on how she'd respond if he touched her elsewhere.

She'd probably slap him silly.

"Are you coming?" she called without looking back.

He grinned and picked up his duffel bag. "Yes, ma'am," he called, and started towards her.

He always had liked a challenge.

Three

By the time the floured chicken was spitting in the grease in the cast iron skillet, Summer felt she had herself back under control. Sure, she'd reacted to the man. No shame there, she told herself, humming as she held her hand under the faucet and washed sticky, egg-batter paste from her fingers. She was only human, and Chase McGuire was a very sexy man.

Pleased with herself for having acknowledged that fact in a calm, mature manner, she patted her hand against the towel hanging next to the sink and headed for the back door.

Her hired hand would need a little notice in order to clean up for supper, one of the two meals a day she owed him. He was probably in the barn. Raul had taken care of the stable chores and left before Summer realized they had rain headed their way. She'd sent Ricky to tell Chase to put up the rest of the horses and close up the box stalls.

That was twenty minutes ago. Ricky was still out there with him.

She frowned as she stepped out on the porch. She wasn't sure she liked the idea of Ricky hanging around Chase McGuire for the next couple of months. The man was apt to stir up Ricky's fascination with the rodeo.

Outside, the air was dusky with storm, the sky, a crisp, exhilarating gray as the day slid into evening. Wind bristled though the leaves on the oaks and made a nuisance of itself by grabbing her hair and throwing it in her face.

She turned toward the barn, and her shirttail flapped in the wind. The flannel rubbed across her bare nipples, and she shivered. She thought about how Chase McGuire had looked at her breasts. Openly. With obvious pleasure.

Somehow she had to figure out a way to get into a bra tomorrow.

None of the horses was out in the paddocks, and all the stalls on this side of the barn were shut to the outside. The southern doorway to the barn glowed a welcoming yellow from the lights Chase must have turned on to fight the premature gloom of the storm-shrouded day.

She paused when she reached the doorway. Neither Chase nor Ricky was in sight, but Dancer's stall door was open. Kelpie lay in front of it, panting happily. Summer headed that way.

"So you got bucked off the first time, huh?" her son's excited voice was saying.

"Sure did. And after all my bragging." A long, mournful sigh, accompanied by the sound of something rubbing rhythmically against wood. "That's when I learned why cowboys are supposed to be strong, silent types. We mostly get ourselves in trouble when we open our mouths. When we aren't bragging, we're putting our foot in it."

Ricky giggled. "Do you put your foot in it?"

"All the time."

Summer stopped in front of the stall next to Kelpie. The dog, exhausted from the day's excitement, settled for standing up and butting her head against Summer's leg. Dancer, a placid old mare Summer used for her beginning riders, munched lazily on her feed in one corner of the stall. On the other side of the stall, Summer's hired hand drew a rasp rhythmically back and forth across a rough, splintery place in one of the wooden supports to the stall while her son watched.

She noticed that his gorgeous black Stetson had been replaced by a beat-up, cream-colored distant cousin—a working cowboy's hat, in fact.

Chase looked up, saw her and smiled the one-dimple smile that fit his face as well as his worn jeans fit his hips. "Looks like you've got a cribber," he said.

A "cribber" was a horse that chewed on whatever wood was around, often swallowing air along with the wood and making itself miserable. "Dancer's not the one with the taste for wood," she said. Her voice came out wrong. She cleared her throat. "It's that blasted gelding of the Bateses, the one who threw me. I moved him to the end stall. It's a little bigger, more room for his toy." She referred to the big ball that rolled around at the horse's feet. Cribbers usually chewed out of boredom, and the ball gave the horse something to do.

"Chase wanted to get the wood smoothed down,"

Ricky broke in, "so's Dancer wouldn't hurt herself on it. We already got all the horses in."

We? "I see," she said. "Well, I'm sure that was a good idea, but, Ricky, you aren't to be following Mr. McGuire around, bothering him with a bunch of questions."

"I wasn't bothering him," Ricky said indignantly. "Was I, Chase?"

"Not a bit." Chase ran the rasp over the wood one last time, then smoothed his fingers over it, testing. "He helped me bring the horses in and then showed me where the tools were so I could get this taken care of."

Summer shifted her feet uncomfortably. The man had found work that needed doing without being told. He was being patient and good-natured with Ricky—and she wished he'd been rude and obnoxious instead. She wished—oh, she didn't know what she wished. She wanted to grab her son and tell him to stay away from Chase McGuire. "Ricky, you know I don't let you handle all of the horses."

He drew his narrow shoulders up straight, offended. "I just got Honey-Do an' Dancer and Mr. Pig and Scooter. Just the ones you always let me get."

Now she'd treated him like a "little kid" in front of his new hero. Summer sighed. "Well, it's time to give me some help now," she said. "Come on up to the house and feed Kelpie, Hannah and Amos." Kelpie yipped when she heard her name, and pushed against Summer's legs again.

"But, Mom, Chase said that he was going to—"

"Ricky," she said once, in her warning voice.

"Yes, ma'am," he said, but his lip stuck out.

"Go ahead and wash up after you feed them," she said. "We're having fried chicken for supper."

That brightened his face again. He looked at Chase. "You don't want to miss Mom's fried chicken, so you prob'ly better get washed up pretty quick, too." Then he took off at his usual dead run with Kelpie running and yipping at his heels.

"Sorry if I kept him from his other chores."

She pulled her eyes away from the barn door her son had disappeared through. Chase stood just where he had before, about four feet away. Not close at all. Maybe her heart gave a little skip when she saw him with his eyes crinkled up at the corners from the smile that never seemed to leave his face. It didn't worry her. The humming in her blood was really rather…pleasant. It was only a natural, physical reaction. "I doubt you had much choice," she said dryly. "I can tell that Ricky's going to be about as hard to detach from you as a burr from a dog's tail. I hope your patience doesn't wear out."

"I like Rick," he said, and walked toward her slow and easy. "He's a bright kid, and he really did help me find where things were. He said the tools were his grandpa's."

Summer felt the little hitch in her breath as he drew closer. He couldn't have heard it, though, which was good. It was best Chase didn't know what effect he had on her.

She turned just a bit suddenly to lead the way out of the stall. "My father left me his tools along with his stable," she said, speaking quickly to distract herself from what she was feeling. "Which was a good thing, since the place wasn't in such great shape when I…he'd been ill," she added, not wanting Chase to think that Sam Erickson would ever have intentionally neglected his property. "He couldn't keep things up very well that last year."

And she'd been gone. Summer's mouth tightened with the familiar ache of reproach. While her father was dying, alone and too proud to tell her about his illness, she'd been following her cowboy husband around the rodeo circuit. She walked a little faster down the aisle between the stalls. "I've got to get back to the house and turn the chicken over. If you'd just shut off the lights when you—"

"Summer." She didn't jump when his hand landed on her shoulder, stopping her. Maybe she'd felt it, had felt him behind her and known he was going to touch her. Maybe…

Gently, he turned her to face him. "No need to gallop off so quick. I'm not going to do a thing you don't want me to do."

Oh, Lord. That's what she was afraid of.

His fingers were callused. She felt them, rough and warm, on her throat, testing the place where her pulse bounded like a doe fleeing the hunter. He *knew,* damn him, and his smiling eyes told her he knew. "After all, you're the boss, aren't you? You're in charge. Everything's got to happen the way you want it to. Right?"

The rafters over their heads creaked in the rising wind. The barn smelled like a barn—like horses and hay—and so did the man in front of her, the man whose fingers rested lightly on the pulse in her throat. All around them horses shuffled their feet, stamped, chewed placidly on whatever remained of their feed, while Summer's muscles softened like wax from the heat of a torch. From just one touch.

And that treacherous smile of his. And the idea, the

sneaky, twisty worm of an idea he'd planted, that she could want, and could have what she wanted.

No. No, she knew where that led. With an effort she pulled back. "It's starting to rain," she said inanely, and turned and walked away. And if she felt him watching her leave—if she knew he was studying the sway of her hips and the shape of her bottom as she moved—she tried very hard not to enjoy the knowledge so damned much.

The air was cool with moonlight and rich with the smell of earth after rain. Chase welcomed the chill as much as the fresh scent. He lay crossways in his too-small bed in the little room off the kennel and looked at the patterns the moonlight made on the ceiling.

He was so hard he hurt. But for the moment, just for the moment, he didn't mind, because it was a good kind of a hurt, an alive kind, the sort he hadn't felt in over a year, not since he woke up in the hospital and realized his days of following the circuit were over. Since then he'd been with a few friendly ladies, but he hadn't really *wanted*.

It was good to want again.

The wind had pretty much departed with the rain, so the shapes the shadow branches made on Chase's ceiling shifted only slightly in the remnants of a breeze. Chase shifted, too, uncomfortable, but not really minding the ache that was keeping him awake.

Chase's temporary quarters were about what he'd expected. The floor was cement, with a rag rug next to the bed. The single window had been painted shut with the same blue paint that was flaking off the chest of drawers, and the closet was the result of someone's less-than-expert carpentry.

But the room was one huge step up from the couch where he'd spent the last two nights. It had a door that he could close when he wanted—or leave open like he had it now. And it was as ruthlessly clean as the tiny bathroom next to it. He supposed the hard-headed woman he worked for must have come in here and scrubbed everything with one hand while he was moving the horses after lunch. She was just not too bright about some things, but Chase was already certain that sort of stubborn, prideful behavior was typical of Summer Callaway.

The storm that had threatened had made an appearance briefly. While he and his pretty boss lady and her son had sat at her kitchen table and eaten fried chicken with oven-fried potatoes, mustard greens drenched in hot sauce and biscuits with butter and honey, the rain had come. It had been one of those quick, noisy cloudbursts, lots of wind and a fast, hard drenching that finished up so abruptly you could just imagine someone upstairs turning off the tap. But while it had lasted...

Eating in the kitchen with a widow woman and her six-year-old son might have made Chase feel itchy. It hadn't. He'd felt comfortable. Maybe, he thought now as he watched the moon shadows, the combination of hot food and him on the inside of four snug walls, with a lot of wind and rain on the outside, was what had made him feel so relaxed and contented. Hard to say. Contentment wasn't a feeling he'd had much experience with.

Chase shifted again in the dark, his skin hot with the same fever that had his groin aching. He shoved the covers off. Chilly night air flowed over his naked body, air freshly washed by the recent rain.

The contentment hadn't lasted. Chase didn't know

what had called up the old memory. Maybe the rain. Maybe it had been the feeling, insidious and terrible, that had snuck in under his guard—that feeling of safety and permanence. Of family. By the time they'd finished eating—and getting in each other's way trying to get the dishes done, since the fool woman wouldn't admit that having only one arm to use hampered her in the slightest—he'd been starting to feel itchy. But it had still been raining, and Ricky had looked awfully hopeful when he'd asked Chase to play checkers.

Probably, he decided, it had been those checkers that did it. Not that Chase had been playing checkers on that other night so many years ago, but they'd played often enough, him and Mike, in that big old ranch house in the first nine years of Chase's life. Enough that the sight of that red-and-black checkerboard had tugged on something inside Chase, something deep and uncomfortable that gave him the urge to get on down the road.

Only he couldn't. He was stuck here for at least two months while he got together enough money to fix his truck. So he'd played checkers.

They were into their second game when he tasted apples.

Apples...sharp, tart and sweet, a taste like the way the wind felt on his skin right now, all crisp and wakeful. Along with the taste, he'd remembered other things. The sound of rain on the roof, not hard and windy like the storm they had tonight, but a steady, soaking rain. The kind of rain ranchers loved. He'd heard that other rain and tasted the apple, and he'd remembered the sight of his brother, Mike, at the table doing homework, one big, square hand holding the other half of the apple Chase was eating. The cuffs on Mike's blue plaid shirt had ended a little too far up his wrists, and his knuckles had been swollen and scabbed from the fight he'd gotten into a couple days before. At fifteen, Mike had been big for his age, and halfway wild. Especially after their mom had moved out.

Chase had remembered the sound of the doorbell ringing. It had rung once that night. Just once.

He'd made some excuse and left Summer and her son in their cozy little house, left while the wind was still whipping the rain around like it had someplace better to be. He'd reached the dark, impersonal haven of the kennel and his room here, and he'd spent the next twenty minutes using his pocket knife to chip off the paint that sealed the window shut. There was no way he'd have been able to sleep knowing he couldn't open that window.

Of course, he reflected as he looked up at his shadowed ceiling, as it turned out he still hadn't been able to sleep. But that was because he'd been thinking about a pretty sunshine woman in the house so nearby. A woman with full breasts and narrow hips and a pouty mouth that she tried her darnedest to keep primmed up and proper.

Summer sure didn't want to want him, Chase thought as he smiled up at his ceiling. But she did.

He meant to have her, right here in this hard, narrow bed. Summer made him come alive in a way he hadn't felt in a long, long time. The best thing he could give her in return, he figured, was some of what she made him feel. She could distract him from the tight, trapped feeling he got from knowing he couldn't throw his bag in the truck and take off whenever he wanted, and he could make her forget about that fool husband of hers. The one who'd promised her forever and then left her, over and over, for the rodeo and the groupies who flocked after the rodeo cowboys.

Chase knew Summer looked at him and thought about her wandering husband, and he knew it had nothing to do with looks. Jimmie had been dark and lean as a whip, with regular features in a face just this side of pretty. And while Chase knew perfectly well that women liked him, it sure wasn't because of his pretty face.

But he wasn't Jimmie Callaway. He wouldn't lie to her, and he wouldn't break any promises, because he wouldn't give her any. And he was only going to leave her once.

"But you didn't ride bulls?" Ricky asked again.

Chase glanced down and smiled as his hands automatically washed, rinsed and stacked another in the endless pile of stainless steel dog dishes. The boy's disappointment was as plain to see as the freckles that marched across his nose and cheeks.

It was late in the afternoon on his first full day of employment at Three Oaks. He and Ricky stood side by side at the big sink at the back of the kennel. The boy had come hurrying to join Chase as soon as he got home from school, but was obviously less than impressed with Chase at the moment.

First off, Ricky didn't consider washing dog bowls a properly macho activity. Then Chase said he'd won all his buckles in saddle bronc and bareback, not bull riding. Bull riders had a certain mystique with the fans, even if a lot of other rodeo folk considered them not overburdened with sense or sanity.

Ricky's dad had been a bull rider. Chase figured the boy was entitled to hold on to a bit of that mystique,

since some of the facts about the event—and about Jimmie Callaway—weren't so appealing.

"When I was first starting on the circuit I rode a few
bulls," he admitted. "I was young and didn't know
better. Even got up on Bodacious once," he said, referring to a huge bull, famous for the extremely short
rides he gave the cowboys who drew him.

"Yeah?" Apparently remembering his offer to help,
the boy grabbed one of the bowls, swiped it twice with
a towel almost as wet as the bowl and set it down. "Did
you make it to the buzzer?"

"Nope." Chase grinned, thinking of that particular
rodeo up in Billings eight years ago. "He got rid of me
right out of the chute. I cracked a couple ribs and
couldn't ride worth a—worth a flip, the rest of the rodeo. Didn't make back my entry fee that time. And
that," he said as he rinsed and stacked the last of the
dog bowls, "is one reason I quit bull riding. You ever
heard of Jim Shoulders?"

"Sure. Uncle Billy talks about him sometimes. He
set lots of records back in the old days, didn't he?"

Chase nodded. He wondered if Summer knew how
much "Uncle Billy," the bull-riding husband of one of
Jimmie Callaway's sisters, figured in Ricky's conversation. "Looks like we're finished up here. I'm going
to head over to the barn and put that paint of your
mother's through his paces. Want to come?"

"Okay." The way Ricky's face lit up let Chase know
he hadn't damaged his standing with the boy too badly.

Because Chase needed to exchange the rubber-soled
shoes he wore in the kennel for his boots, he stopped
by his room first. "Jim Shoulders," he said as he got
a pair of clean socks from the drawer, "set a record for
earnings on bulls that lasted for twenty years, and might

still be the top figure if it were adjusted for inflation. You want to know what he said about how to ride a bull?'' He sat on the bed.

''Sure.'' This was the first time the boy had been in the room since Chase had moved in. He circled it now, looking over Chase's meager belongings with the open curiosity of the young while Chase pulled off his socks, damp from hosing the dog runs down with chlorine water. His pretty boss lady had a couple pairs of rubber boots—hers and a pair that had been her father's—but Chase's feet were too big for either one.

''He said the trick was to put one leg on each side of a bull and make an ugly face for eight seconds.''

Ricky laughed. There was something, Chase reflected, mighty appealing about the way a kid's laughter sounded. He thought of his niece and smiled. ''Now, I was pretty good at making an ugly face, the good Lord having given me a head start on it, and I managed the part about getting my legs on either side of the bull just fine. But that darned eight seconds kept tripping me up.''

Ricky flashed him a grin and stopped by the window. The day was sunny, and so warm for January Chase never considered getting a jacket. Light streamed through the window glass and through Chase's rainbow sun catcher and tossed a second, shimmery rainbow on the cement floor.

Ricky's curious touch set both rainbows to bobbing. ''Mom says bull riding is stupid,'' the boy said. ''She says that for a grown man to get on the back of a ton of angry bull doesn't show the sense God gave a goose. But,'' Ricky said, setting the sun catcher to dancing with another touch, ''I think she's down on rodeo 'cause of my dad. He died, you know.''

"Oh?" Not sure what to say, Chase busied himself with pulling the first boot on.

"Yeah. I was just little when it happened, so I don't remember." He left the window to stand in front of the small chest of drawers with the peeling blue paint. "Hey, isn't this from the NFR?" Ricky picked up the big gold belt buckle Chase had set on top of the chest.

"Yeah."

Ricky studied the buckle. "Mom used to rodeo, too, a long time ago. She was a barrel racer, but my grandpa didn't want her to because he was an old fussbudget an' his shorts were too tight. That's what Aunt Maud says. So Mom liked rodeo OK at first, but then my dad died and she didn't like it anymore." He set the buckle down carefully. "How come you don't rodeo anymore?"

Chase pulled the second boot on. "Nothing lasts forever." He'd forgotten that, though, hadn't he? He'd forgotten he wouldn't be able to ride broncs forever, so he had only himself to blame if giving that up had taken something out of him. Something important.

Ricky pointed at the framed photo on the chest. In it, a dark-haired man smiled at a four-year-old girl wearing a lacy dress and a big grin. "Who's that?"

"My brother, Mike, and his little girl. Her name's Jennifer."

"What's that she's got on her legs?"

"Braces. She needs those to help her walk." Chase stood and stamped his feet down into the boots, wondering about that younger Summer, the one who "used to rodeo."

"How come?"

"When Jennifer was born, some of her bones weren't shaped quite right."

"So do those braces get her bones right?"

The voice from the doorway was exasperated. "Richard Samuel Callaway. You know what I've told you about being nosy about people who look different than you expect them to."

Chase turned his head. Summer stood in the doorway, cradling an old, black dial telephone in her good arm and looking embarrassed. She'd tied her hair back that morning, or tried to. Half of it had freed itself of the scarf. Her jeans were old and sagged at the knees. Her button-down knit shirt was old and a slightly darker blue than her sling and, unfortunately, not at all tight. Still, he was pretty sure she was braless again.

How crass of him to take pleasure from something she couldn't help. He grinned.

"Yeah, but she's not here, Mom," Ricky said reasonably, "so it can't make her feel bad, can it?"

"But her uncle *is* here, and you were asking some very nosy questions." She tossed her head, trying to get some of her hair back out of her face.

"Yeah, but—"

"Besides which, you didn't make your bed this morning. You have any money, buster?"

He heaved a big, put-upon sigh. "I s'pose you want me to pay the penalty box."

"*And* make up your bed."

Ricky lingered long enough to assure Chase he'd join him at the barn as soon as he got his stupid bed made, then took off at typical little-boy speed.

"I'm sorry about the way he keeps pestering you," Summer said, and absently lifted both phone and arm so she could tuck some of that freedom-loving hair of hers back behind her ear. "I'm afraid I'd have to tie him up in his room to keep him away."

"No need to get out the rope," Chase said. "Rick's good company." He smiled at the way she was looking at him, all wary and preoccupied. One end of the phone's cord dangled down, kind of like the hair she kept messing with. "If you're expecting a call, you probably ought to plug that thing in."

She looked startled, like she'd forgotten what she was holding. "Oh, I—no, I just thought—this is for you." She shoved the phone at him. He stepped forward to take it, then stayed where he was, close enough to breath in some faint scent that drifted up from her. "Since I've usually got the cordless with me," she explained, and if her voice was a little breathless, her eyes stayed cautious. "There's a wall jack in here somewhere that you could plug this one into. So you could make calls if you wanted."

"Thanks," he said softly. He wondered if she knew the phone was an excuse. She could have given it to him at supper. She hadn't had to come after him here. "I won't put any long distance calls on it."

"I'm not worried about that." Her eyes fled his for a moment, going to the photo on the dresser. "But if you did want to call your brother or something, I could take the charges out of your pay."

So she'd heard that much, had she? "I've already written Mike a letter. Handed it to the postman today."

"Well, that's good." Her tongue came out and licked her lips nervously. "I also wanted to let you know that it's okay if you need to use the pickup sometimes. I've got my car, so you wouldn't be doing me out of transportation or anything. I know it's hard—" she faltered when he eased closer "—hard to be trapped someplace without transportation. So just let me know if you want to use it. For a beer or something."

He was making her uneasy, was he? Chase smiled. "That's a mighty thoughtful offer." What was the scent that drifted up to him from her? "How's that shoulder of yours?"

"Oh…not bad. I probably should have gone ahead with the lessons today."

"No, you did right to wait on those until next week." Her scent made him think of hot days and blue skies and whipped cream. "The collarbone will still be a problem then, but your shoulder should be better." He lifted one hand and gently tucked some of that bothersome hair behind her ear. His thumb made a single stroke along her jaw, then underneath, to the fragile place in her throat where her pulse throbbed.

He felt her heartbeat pick up.

He let his fingertips drift down the strand he'd just rearranged. "I gave Mike your phone number, in case he needs to get in touch with me for something. I hope you don't mind."

"No. No, of course not."

"You sure are good to your hired hand…ma'am." He took the strand of hair and lifted it to his face.

Her brows drew down, tucking a little vee in between them. "What are—"

"Strawberries," he said, inhaling and rubbing her hair between his fingers. It was silky soft. "Your hair smells like strawberries."

"It's…my shampoo." The frown stayed hitched to her eyebrows, but she didn't move. When he took the strand of hair and feathered it along her cheek and throat, teasing her with it, she stood very still, barely breathing. Even when he brushed her lightly, lightly along the skin exposed by her blue shirt, down to the beginning swell of her breasts, she didn't move.

She wanted touching. Oh, he knew her need, felt it in her almost as strongly as he felt the pulse of his own blood in his fingertips and in his groin, the quickly mounting ache. How long had it been, he wondered, since she was touched?

Their eyes caught and held. Hers were as blue and hot as the sky he'd been thinking of, and gave him the strangest sense of vertigo—like when, as a boy, he would lie on his back and stare up at the sky for so long he felt like he might fall right up into it.

She shivered.

He reached for the first button on her shirt...and the phone rang.

They both jumped. Chase stared, disbelieving, at the unplugged black phone he still held under his arm. Summer laughed. It was shaky, but it was a laugh.

"It's this one," she said, and her hand went to her sling. She pulled the cordless phone out.

When she greeted the caller, her voice was almost normal. Her first few words told him it was someone she knew well—a neighbor, it sounded like, and not an especially friendly one, judging by the way she was apologizing for Ricky having been on the man's land.

Summer met his eyes briefly before turning and heading back out toward the office. Her expression told him she was back in control, back behind those fences she thought she needed.

But she was thinking about him. He'd seen that, too, in her eyes—the unmistakable glint of feminine speculation. She was wondering what would have happened if the phone hadn't rung. He smiled in spite of the demands his body made that he follow her, hold her, press himself against her—do *something*.

His body would have to go unsatisfied a while

longer. Though some people might have been amazed to hear it, Chase was unused to seducing women. He was having to figure out how to do it as he went along. Seduction implied unwillingness, and Chase had never wasted his time or troubled his conscience with unwilling women.

Coaxing was different. Women, however willing, liked to be coaxed, and Chase had always enjoyed giving them reasons to do what they wanted to do.

But Summer wasn't willing, not really, in spite of how hungry she was for a man's touch. Chase knew it. He'd have to gentle her as carefully as ever he'd gentled a two-year-old filly, who had to be persuaded, first, to accept the weight of a saddle before he got her used to his own weight in the saddle. And strangely enough, in spite of the discomfort of his body and the guilty silence from where his conscience used to be, he didn't mind waiting for her, working to have her.

Summer was thinking about him and what he made her feel. That was enough for now.

Four

Summer was no fool. She stayed away from Chase McGuire the next day, leaving him alone in the kitchen when he ate lunch, avoiding the kennel while he was there.

Ricky, of course, did just the opposite once he came home from school. So it wasn't Summer's fault that she had to go looking for her hired hand that afternoon around five-thirty. Ricky had ducked outside without doing his homework.

She knew where he was. Chase had come to the kitchen earlier, while she was trying to assemble lasagna one-handed. She'd handled the encounter well, she thought as she stepped out onto the porch, nodding to herself in approval. She'd been as pleasant and cool as the weather today. When she'd asked what he needed, he'd said he was going to *longe* the Bateses' gelding before trying to ride him, and did she want to watch?

Of course she'd said she was too busy. So, while his wicked eyes laughed at her for avoiding him, he asked if she had any advice about the gelding.

"Don't get bucked off," she'd told him dryly.

"I try not to let that happen every time," he'd said with a surprising bite in his voice.

She wondered now, as she headed across the yard, if he'd thought she was laughing at him rather than herself. Summer hadn't kept up with rodeo much in the past couple years, so she didn't know what had happened to leave one of its golden boys stranded in a tiny town, broke and badly in need of a job. Had he been bucked off so many times he gave up on competing, or did his bitterness have something to do with whatever made him limp?

Summer could have reached the *longeing* pen from the outside, but preferred to go through the stable so she could check on its occupants and assure herself that all was well. The air inside was warm and redolent with the comforting odors of horses, hay and manure. Halfway up the main aisle was a narrow passage that led to the *longeing* pen. As she neared it she heard the rhythmic thud of horse hooves on the packed earth in the pen, a sound as solid and satisfying to her as the swishing of tails and crunching of grain in the stalls she passed.

She paused in the doorway, watching. Ricky was perched on the side of the two-rail fence nearest her—without, she noticed with a sigh, the windbreaker she'd made sure he had on earlier. A stocky chestnut gelding with a white blaze and three white stockings loped around the perimeter of the fenced area, circling the man in the center. Chase turned with the horse's circuit, the yellow-and-white *longe* line stretched between them moving like the second hand of a clock. He held the whip in his left hand, six feet of handle with about the same amount of lash.

Something about him looked different. After a moment she understood why. He wasn't smiling.

Curious, she moved up to the fence beside Ricky.

"Hi, Mom," he said without looking away from Chase. He was, as usual, wrinkled and rumpled everywhere but his hair. Silky-smooth as a horse's muzzle, it fell in dark bangs across his forehead.

"Hi, yourself. Do the words *math* and *homework* mean anything to you?"

He grinned. "Nope, not a thing."

The muscles in her cheek twitched with the effort of not grinning back. Because she knew he'd hate it if she brushed his hair out of his eyes the way she wanted to, she put her hands on the fence. The top rail was chest high to her, cool and rough beneath her palm as she gripped it and watched the man and horse together.

Focus. Everything about Chase spoke of it. Beneath the brim of his old cream hat, his eyes tracked each movement of the horse. He moved with quiet readiness, his entire attention on the horse loping at the other end of the *longe* line he held. She had no idea if he even knew she was there.

"Maverick's behaving awfully well," she said in low-voiced surprise.

"Not at first. He's tried to bite Chase, and he's tried to kick him, but Chase doesn't let him get away with a thing," Ricky said, as proudly as if he'd invented the man.

Summer felt an unpleasant little wriggle that she recognized as jealousy. Was she so petty that she didn't want Ricky to look up to anyone but her? "Home-work," she reminded her son.

"Aw, Mom..."

She raised her eyebrows. "I thought we had a deal."

Ricky hesitated, torn between watching Chase work Maverick now and watching the cartoons on Saturday morning, an interminable three days away. Finally he jumped down. "Aren't you coming?"

She should, shouldn't she? But she'd never seen Chase like this. Serious. Absorbed. There was some-thing here she didn't understand, and she needed to. "In a minute," she said, giving in to the urge to brush Ricky's hair out of his eyes.

Predictably, he made a face and pulled away.

"Get your jacket from wherever you left it," she called to his retreating form. Then she turned back.

Chase turned in slow circles, the stiffness in his bad leg almost invisible. The sight of him working the horse made her feel strange—unsettled and yet, in some cor-ner of her heart, pleased. Summer would have argued with anyone who called her life as a single woman in-complete, yet there was satisfaction in seeing a man here, where she'd watched her father work horses so many times in the past.

Maverick broke stride. He tossed his head, rolling his eyes—declarations of independence that would, she knew, be quickly followed by a charge at the man who dared tell him what to do. Before the horse could act on his challenge, though, the whip's thong snapped loudly just behind his rump. The horse jumped forward and resumed his steady lope. Chase's expression never altered.

Summer loved horses, loved working with them, and she was good at it. Within five minutes of watching the way this man and horse moved together, she knew Chase was better than good. Far better.

This thought brought no disturbing hint of jealousy. Summer knew her skills had more to do with affection and experience than any touch of genius, but she'd seen a couple of trainers so touched—people with an uncanny ability to understand and anticipate the animals. She hadn't known a former bronc rider could own both the patience and the rapport that went into making a world-class trainer.

Fascinated, she kept watching.

Longeing a horse served several functions, but with the high-spirited gelding the main idea was to get him used to obeying while tiring him out enough to lose interest in hijinks. Horses on the *longe* line were controlled by the noise of the whip and by the sight of it, long and menacing, able to reach them even when the irritating human was yards away. No decent handler ever let the whip actually touch a horse, much less used it to hurt.

Jimmie had. Once. The memory came to Summer unwilled.

He'd been home for a month that time, while his ribs healed. Jimmie had never been one to take his moods out on her or Ricky. She gave him that much credit. So she'd had no idea that he might take them out on the horses, in the guise of helping her out at the stable while he was home. When she'd seen him that day in the *longe* pen, the last haziness of love had evaporated, leaving her vision clear. She'd seen a frustrated boy in the body of a man, a boy used to subduing horses, conquering them, in the arena. When he actually lashed a stubborn horse of hers with the *longe* whip, she'd gone a little crazy.

Chase gave the gelding the signal to slow—a verbal cue accompanied by a tug on the line. The horse, tired now from his exercise, was glad enough to drop into a trot. The obedience didn't affect Chase's expression any more than the misbehavior had. He remained confident, in control.

Summer thought of her father. Sam Erickson had never been one for emotional displays, either of approval or condemnation, but he'd expected obedience from his horses...and his daughter.

But Chase didn't withhold approval. He murmured low and soft to Maverick about what a good horse the gelding was, how clever, how strong, and a small, aching place woke inside Summer. And she realized abruptly that Chase wasn't like her father, no more than he was really like Jimmie.

The realization was as unasked for and unwelcome as any intruder. All she could think of to do was leave. Summer took a step away.

"I'll be through in a minute," Chase said, his voice as soft as if he were speaking to the horse.

Slowly she turned. Slowly, reluctantly, she said, "You're very good."

One corner of his mouth turned up, tucking that dimple of his into his cheek—but his eyes were all for the horse, trotting sedately now. "Yeah, I am. Want to see me do a handstand?"

"Have you thought of training professionally? You must have some connections, and with your talent—"

"Too much responsibility," he said lightly. "I just play around at it sometimes. I'm glad you changed your mind and decided to watch, though. It gave me a chance to impress you."

"I didn't change my mind," she said sharply. "I

came to tell Ricky to do his homework and to let you know that supper will be ready in about forty minutes.''

For just a moment he looked away from the horse. His eyes, steady and slightly amused, met hers. And maybe she knew how Maverick felt, because he didn't have to speak. She heard his taunt quite clearly: *Liar*.

She didn't speak, either, when she turned and left.

Six days and six restless nights later, the South Texas version of a cold front blew in. Beneath a sullen sky the earth was a monochrome—black where a recent shower left the tree trunks and patches of dirt dark and wet, gray everywhere else. The air was a snappish forty-one degrees. February had come creeping in a few days ago, and even in the San Antonio area, winter bared its teeth now and again.

Of course, to a man raised in Montana, they were puppy teeth.

To a woman raised in Bita Creek, winter's bite was invigorating. The chilly weather made Summer want to ride so badly she could taste it.

Instead, she did laundry. ''I really do appreciate this, Maud,'' Summer said as she followed her tiny friend out onto the back porch, her right arm full of sheets. The shoulder that had been dislocated no longer bothered her, but the sling helped keep her collarbone still so it could mend faster.

Kept it from hurting so much, too. She hadn't needed a pain pill to help her sleep in over a week, but she still had at least two and a half weeks of not being able to do much of anything and four weeks or more before she could use both sides of her body normally. It was driving her crazy.

''You hate it,'' Maud corrected with one of her raspy

chuckles. "It purely galls you to accept any help. You're like your father that way."

Summer grimaced. "I'm not sure that's a compliment."

"It's not," Maud said as they turned the corner on the big, wraparound porch that skirted two sides of her little frame house.

Summer couldn't argue. Her father had been so blasted independent he'd failed to tell his only child—his only near kin of any kind—about his cancer. If Summer hadn't left the circuit after she'd gotten pregnant, she might not have seen him at all before he died.

The buzzer on the dryer was calling. Maud gave Summer a reproachful look as she reached for the screen door to the covered portion of the porch. "Started already, did you? I told you at church Sunday I was coming over to help."

Summer was embarrassed. "I just tossed some towels and things in earlier." She followed Maud through the screen door.

Summer's "laundry room" was on her side porch. When Summer was seven, her father had screened in the west end. When she was fourteen he'd plumbed it so he could move the washing machine out of the kitchen. It had soon been joined by a dryer—a purchase that had thrilled Summer, since she was doing all the laundry by then. She'd since replaced both appliances and added several potted plants and a small space heater, but hadn't felt the need to change anything else.

She'd made few changes of any sort since inheriting Three Oaks, actually, except for necessary repairs and some modernization at the stable. The porch was still painted gray, because that was the color the hardware store in Bita Creek stocked for porch paint, and because gray was a proper sort of color for a porch. Frame houses like hers were supposed to be white, and while she had toyed with the idea of using blue shingles instead of green when she had to get the roof replaced four years ago, in the end she'd vetoed such a frivolous notion.

As soon as the screen door banged shut behind her she reached for the radio. Garth Brooks started singing his latest country tune.

"So how's that gorgeous hired hand of yours working out?" Maud asked, setting the laundry basket down by the washer and bending down to turn the little electric heater on.

Summer shot her a suspicious glance as she dumped the dirty sheets on the floor and reached for the dryer door. "He's a hard worker," she said neutrally.

"Not much like Jimmie, after all, is he?" Maud said, looking pleased. "Here, let me fold while you get the next load started. Folding's better done with two arms."

Summer relaxed when Maud let her turn the conversation toward local affairs. She liked the porch better than a regular utility room. Out here she had breezes in summer, the smell of growing things in spring and a roof in winter. She could look down the road at Maud's place, or across the pasture toward the creek, while she washed, folded, ironed and hung up clothes.

Maud told her about a couple from church who'd split up and another who had reconciled and about the son of some other neighbors who'd been arrested for DWI the night before last and was worrying his poor parents "plumb to death."

"Ida over to the drugstore thinks Curtis may reconsider that offer Ray Fletcher made him," Maud said as she plugged in the iron. "Maybe if he got his son away from the Harlowe twins he could get that boy straightened out.''

''Ida likes the sound of her own voice too much. She doesn't really know anything.'' Summer hated the idea of Fletcher getting a toehold in the community. So far, Bita Creek's rural character hadn't been changed too much by the few city people who'd moved there, either permanently or as weekend residents. But Fletcher's plans called for upscale condos, a couple of small, ritzy restaurants and all sorts of things that would drive property taxes up even more and change her hometown in ways that made her stomach clench.

''Don't be such an old fogie. Change isn't always a bad thing.'' Maud licked her fingertip and touched it to the iron, testing it. ''Pass me one of Ricky's shirts.''

''I am not an old fogie,'' Summer said, propping her hand on her hip. ''And I can handle an iron perfectly well with one hand, Maud. You aren't—''

''Go make us some coffee,'' Maud said, bending to get one of the shirts herself. ''And when you come back I'll tell you what Will Stafford told me about your hired hand.''

Summer hesitated, aggravated, but aware that the old woman was having a wonderful time taking over. Everyone needs to be needed, she reminded herself. ''All right,'' she said. ''But I don't really care what Will Stafford said.''

Both of Maud's scraggly, white eyebrows went up. ''You don't, huh? It doesn't matter to you how Chase McGuire got his knee so banged up he had to quit rodeoing?''

Summer tried to stare Maud down, but her mouth twitched. She gave up and laughed, mostly at herself. ''Oh, all right. I'll go make coffee, and I'll even admit

that I'm curious about Chase's injury. Are you satisfied?''

''Not yet,'' Maud murmured as the screen door
closed behind Summer, a smile on her wrinkled face
when she turned back to the ironing board. ''Not yet,
but you're doing better.''

Fifteen minutes later Summer let the back door slam
behind her, since both her hands were full. She carried
the coffeepot in her good hand and hooked the handles
of two mugs with the fingers of her other hand.

As soon as she turned the corner on the porch, she
realized Maud wasn't alone. Chase's laugh sounded low
and confidential, practically flirtatious. ''You're something else, Maudie, you know that?''

Maudie? Summer made a face. ''Can someone get
the door?'' she said as she reached the screen.

Chase opened it, of course. He stood there looking
entirely too good in his faded jeans and a long-sleeved
shirt that had been a bright green many washings ago.
He'd set his hat down, and his hair was the color of
sunshine on winter hay, while his smile was the
warmest thing she'd seen all day.

She frowned at him. ''I only brought two cups.''

He reached to take the coffeepot from her. ''A good
hostess like you is bound to be upset about a little over-
sight like that, but don't let it bother you,'' he said,
flashing his dimple at her. ''I can go get another one.''

''Summer doesn't mind fetching another cup one
bit,'' Maud informed them both.

She shot Maud a wry look. ''No, I don't. Not a bit.
Here.'' She handed Chase the cups. ''Help yourself,
and I'll go get another one.''

He laid his hand on her arm, stopping her. ''Wait. I

shouldn't have teased you. I can't stay for coffee. I came to tell you…well,'' he said, glancing at Maud and setting the pot and cups down on the table near the door, "maybe it's better if I show you. Can you come to the stable?''

Go with him to the stable, when she'd been avoiding spending any time alone with him? She shook her head. "I could, but why don't you just tell me?''

"Because you'd insist on going to see for yourself, anyway,'' he said. "You're not likely to take my unsupported opinion about bad news.''

Her heart jerked in her chest, and she reached out to clutch his arm. "The horses? Which of them—''

"No,'' he said quickly, "not the horses. They're all fine. This is the 'it's going to cost money' sort of bad news.''

She grimaced and let her hand fall. She was all too familiar with that sort.

"Well,'' said Maud, bending over to shut off the space heater, "let's go.''

Chase grinned. "Now, Maudie, I bet a few years back you'd have been at the top of my list of ladies to sweet-talk up into the stable loft, but I think maybe you'd better stay on the ground this time.''

"As if I'd have gone up in a loft with the likes of you,'' Maud said with a sniff, looking delighted. "Oh, go on, both of you.''

Summer walked across the yard next to her hired hand. His limp was worse, and she wondered if the cold weather affected it. Or had he done something to aggravate it? The curiosity she felt was as irritating as a mosquito bite. She blamed it on Maud, for bringing the subject up. "You and Maud seem to be getting along like a house afire,'' she said.

"She's trying to talk me into something." He chuckled. "You, to be specific. She thinks I ought to, uh, court you."

"Oh, Lord," she muttered. That's all she needed, Maud playing matchmaker while Chase counted the days until he could move on down the road. Summer already spent her days staying away from this man with his private smiles and roving hands, while her nights were filled with restless dreams.

Staying away wasn't easy. No, keeping her distance took effort, and walking beside him now felt as natural and dangerously exhilarating as it had once felt to sit the back of a horse racing flat-out between barrels. Which was reason enough to keep her distance. Summer knew herself much better now than she had at eighteen.

But, whispered a small voice as they neared the stable, *I'm not eighteen anymore.* Maybe she could handle these feelings now—hot, bubbling feelings that pushed and pushed at her, like lava welling up from some hidden center. Maybe she was mature enough now to deal with the ache and the cravings in the way a lot of other women did.

"So is whatever you want to show me up in the loft?" she asked abruptly. "Or was that just part of your flirting with Maud?"

"It's in the loft." He didn't sound amused now.

She glanced at him just as they left the chilly sunshine of the yard for the dimmer light and warmth in the stable. His expression was shadowed, hard to read. Her heart beat too fast, accelerated by anxiety over why he'd brought her here, and by a feeling she didn't want to acknowledge but couldn't ignore: the compulsion to touch.

Oh, yes, she did want to touch him. She wanted to trace those creases in his face left by his frequent smiles, or skim her fingertips over the veins in the backs of his hands. He had a workingman's hands, the skin dark from the sun and rough from his labor, with half a dozen little nicks and cuts and scars scattered over them.

Did she really think she could handle that, too? Could she touch and be touched without having it matter?

She stopped dead at the foot of the ladder to the loft, with him right behind her.

"Do you need some help?"

Yes, she thought, feeling like a fool because she was reacting to him like a mare in heat—or like a lonely widow too long without a man, which was even more embarrassing. "No," she said. "I don't need two arms for the ladder."

The roof must be leaking, she thought as she climbed the ladder ahead of him. What else could he want her to see in the loft? She stored a few odds and ends up here in addition to the alfalfa hay, but the roof was the only really high-dollar item, and he'd warned her this was an expensive problem.

As soon as she stood on the slatted floor of the loft, she knew why he'd wanted her to see for herself. "Oh, no." She hurried forward.

The bales of hay had been shifted out of their neat stacks, and their new positions revealed the ominous gray of mold on them.

"I think the mold has spread to pretty much all of it," he said grimly, "except for those two." He nodded at two bales that sat separate from all the rest.

Two bales? Two bales untouched, out of all she'd

bought last month? Summer had to check for herself, going from one bale to another, laying her hand on any that didn't look obviously contaminated. The bales where mold grew unseen were hot to the touch, and the musty smell was unpleasantly distinctive.

She noticed something else. Toward the middle of the loft, where the bales had been thickly stacked before Chase started moving them, the floorboards were dark and damp looking.

Alfalfa hay, unlike grass hay, molded when wet.

Moldy hay caused colic.

Colic killed horses.

She knelt. The wood *was* damp. She shook her head, trying to understand. "How could the roof have leaked this badly without anyone noticing?"

"There's no leak, Summer. It looks like someone soaked everything down with the hose two or three weeks ago," Chase said from behind her. "Given the rainy weather you've had this month, the hay had no chance of drying. As for who it was—well, you could guess about that better than me."

"It was intentional." She said it, but could hardly believe it. She rose slowly, wiping her hands off on her jeans as if she could wipe off the taint of enmity. "Someone wet the hay down on purpose." She looked around, unable to think of what she was supposed to *do*. Someone had played a vicious trick on her, and she didn't understand. "What do I do now?" she heard herself ask, bewildered. "There isn't any alfalfa hay at the feed store. It's been too wet to bale."

"You've got friends with horses or ranches around here, don't you?"

Summer shook her head, disoriented still. Someone had done this *on purpose*. She couldn't get past that.

"None of them are going to have much alfalfa hay to sell. The younger horses can get by with grass hay, but the older ones, like Honey-Do, need the alfalfa." Then she exclaimed, "Why would anyone do such a thing? What if some of this had been given to the horses?"

"I think," he said quietly as he came up behind her, "you have to assume that was the goal."

She turned to face him. "No," she said vehemently. "No, that doesn't make sense. Moldy hay can *kill* a horse."

"I know," he said gently.

Of course he knew that. Anyone who knew anything at all about horses knew that. All at once she shivered. "No one I know would do that, kill a horse just to get to me. I don't have any enemies who would do such a thing."

"Not an enemy, maybe, but someone with another sort of motive. Like that developer."

"Ray Fletcher is a sorry son of a gun, but why would he do this? The hay will cost me a couple hundred to replace, and that hurts, but it won't force me to sell the land. Besides, he doesn't know beans about horses, and how would he get up here? Hannah sounds the alarm the minute he sets foot in the yard."

"He could have had help," Chase said, "from someone who does know horses, someone who—oh, hell, don't look like that, Summer. Here." And without even asking he put his hands on her and pulled her up against him.

"I'm fine," she told his shirt, her heart pounding a mile a minute, her hands curled tightly into fists that rested against his chest. "You don't have to comfort me. I'm just—"

"Fine. I know." He started rubbing her back.

"You're in peachy-keen shape and you don't need anyone, but just shut up and let me pretend to be useful here for a minute, okay?"

His hand made slow, soothing circles on her back. She opened her mouth to argue with him and out came a jerky little hiccup—and then she didn't dare speak, because the hiccup meant she was appallingly close to crying.

Chase was more than half a head taller than her, which meant that her head fit perfectly into the place between his shoulder and his chin. He smelled warm and good, but when she took a deep breath it caught on something right in the middle—not a sob, no. Whatever she'd inhaled along with his scent made her dizzy, but it banished her tears entirely.

So she stood very still and let him hold her and rub those soothing circles on her back with his big hand. Even though she didn't feel like crying anymore, she thought she would burst into tears if she tried to pull away at just that moment—which made no sense, no sense at all. And the only reason her heart was pounding so hard was because—but she couldn't think of a reason, no reason at all...except for the truth.

"I can deal with this," she murmured.

"Of course you can," he said.

Summer knew he was talking about the moldy hay, which she should have been talking about, too. She grieved for herself and her treacherous feelings, and tried to be glad that he intended only comfort, while she was burning alive in his arms, because it was safer this way. Safer must surely be better.

Then he moved. His hands slid from her back to her waist to her buttocks and scooped her firmly up against him, and in the same second that she felt the hard evidence of how wrong she'd been about his intentions, those hands went to her face and tilted her head back.

He smiled down into her astonished eyes—at least his mouth was smiling. But there was a mystery in his eyes, something both more and less than a smile. "You shouldn't have trusted me, should you? I meant well, but I'm no good at resisting temptation, Summer, no good at all. You really should remember that."

Then he bent his head and kissed her.

No, she said, but the word stayed inside and her eyes drifted shut. She didn't want to let him in, wasn't going to let him in, but his mouth was wise and patient, nibbling at hers, teaching her to be still, to wait quietly and let him do this…and this…until she had to let her lips part so her panting breaths could get out. Then his tongue came inside.

She shuddered. The wave that surged through her, lava hot and elemental, must have taken him, too. Because suddenly he wasn't patient. One hand tightened at her nape and the other pulled her hard against him. She made a sound deep in her throat, a hungry, craving sound, and helped him get her body closer to his.

They both forgot her collarbone.

The sound she made was as muffled as her hungry moan had been, but he must have recognized the difference between pain and passion immediately. He jerked his head up and dropped his hands.

Instinctively she stepped back. Her mind blank, she stared at him, the throbbing in the middle of her shoulder less fierce than the throbbing elsewhere in her body. The signs of his arousal did nothing to quiet her own. His eyes were hooded. His mouth was wet from hers, and the rapid rise and fall of his chest matched her own hasty breathing.

A cocky smile started in his eyes and traveled quickly to his lips. Summer looked at his smug, smiling face for one long, unthinking second.

Then she punched him in the stomach.

Five

At five o'clock that afternoon the sun hung a few hand spans above the western horizon, a hard, cold ball in a gunmetal sky. In the big exercise paddock, three pint-size riders and one slightly taller one provided the only color in the scene. Their jackets ranged from hot pink to camouflage green, and their mounts ranged from a chubby pony barely ten hands high to quiet, old Dancer. The horses' tails waved like flags in the wind that had started up about an hour ago, pushing those gray clouds ahead of it.

More rain was on its way.

In the center of the paddock stood a woman in dusty jeans, a pale blue sling and a sloppy sweater the color of a tomato about to burst from having soaked up so much sun. Her hair—most of it—was tied back in a low ponytail with a frayed yellow scarf.

Summer's shoulder throbbed painfully, and her temper was sparking like the bare end of a hot wire. None of that showed on her face or in her voice as she called out to Davey, reminding him to keep his heels down. She turned in slow circles, watching her four charges on their various steeds—two ponies and two quiet, steady horses.

Old horses. Horses whose digestion couldn't handle grass hay.

When she heard the truck pull up in the yard next to the stable she called out, "Keep them moving for a few minutes, guys. I'll be right back."

The truck Chase climbed out of was a seventeen-year-old Ford, and every one of those years showed on its battered green body. It ran well enough, though, especially since she'd had the engine overhauled last year. Summer saw no reason it shouldn't last another five or ten years.

Chase was bareheaded for once. He glanced at her as she headed his way, but went directly around to the bed, where three small bales of alfalfa hay sat.

She stopped next to the truck, standing where she could keep an eye on her students. "What in the world took you so long?" she demanded. He'd been gone almost three hours. It shouldn't have taken more than one of those hours to pick up the small amount of alfalfa hay an old friend of her father's had been willing to let her buy from his stock.

Chase didn't know exactly what was bothering Summer, but he had a couple pretty good guesses. He vaulted over the tailgate into the bed, then bent to let down the tailgate. "Where I come from, when a neighbor does you a favor you offer to do something in return. Adams was moving stock from one pasture to another, so I stayed and helped a while." Chase had needed the time away, time to cool down. In more ways than one.

She flushed. "Sorry," she muttered. "It's just—oh, damn and blast this hair, anyway," she said when the wind insisted on blowing the loose strands in her face. "Raul didn't show up."

He jerked his gloves from his back pocket and pulled them on. "So how the hell did you get those kids' horses tacked up?"

She held her hair out of her face with one hand. "Ricky took care of their bridles before he went in to do his homework, and Leanne—she's the tallest one, in the pink jacket—was able to lift the saddles, so all I had to do was the girths."

"You don't have any sense at all, do you?" he said, mad and not knowing why. "I don't suppose it occurred to you to call someone and get some help."

"I called Raul. Or tried to." She stopped. He could see her throat work when she swallowed. "His mother said he's gone to work for some garage in a town fifteen miles east of here."

"I see." And he did see. Raul's guilt had been obvious to him from the first, as obvious as Summer's reluctance to believe it.

"He wasn't even going to tell me."

"Did you expect him to? He may not realize you've discovered what he did, but he must have known you'd find out soon. There were only two bales of untouched hay left for him to give the horses." That look on her face, like she was still hurting over Raul's betrayal, got to him. He grabbed one of the bales by the wire binding it, and heaved it off the tailgate a bit harder than necessary.

"We don't know he did it."

Dammit, she couldn't just keep denying the truth indefinitely. He grabbed the next bale. "If he didn't do it himself, how could he have missed noticing that the hay was wet? He's the only one who's been in the loft in the past few weeks, from what you said when you hired me...ma'am."

Oh, that *ma'am* riled her. Good. He followed the bale of hay and hopped down.

She reminded him of a barn cat, the way her hair was straggling out of that scarf, with her chin tilted up as she glared at him. Barn cats had to work for a living, but they had the same go-to-hell haughtiness their pampered, pedigreed cousins were famous for.

Her eyes narrowed. "Don't you feel a little foolish falling back on those phony manners of yours," she said, "after molesting me in the loft?"

"Molesting?" He grinned. He liked her angry much better than bewildered and hurt. "Is that what you call it? If so, then you were doing some pretty fine molesting of your own...ma'am." She looked ready to punch him again. He shook his head, enjoying himself. "I kind of thought, when I saw you headed over here, you might be going to apologize."

"Wh-what?" She sputtered, she was so mad.

He raised his eyebrows. "Why, for hitting me. I'm pretty sure there are rules against that sort of thing— you being my employer and all." He eased a bit closer, holding her eyes with his. "You do pack quite a wallop, boss lady," he said softly. More than she knew. More than he had any intention of letting her know.

He saw the nerves in the way her eyelids dipped and rose, in the quick motion of her throat as she swallowed. But she didn't back down or back off. He suspected Summer would break her other arm and a leg or two before she'd back down, and damn, he couldn't help but admire that kind of blind, stupid stubbornness, having a touch of the same quality himself.

''We'd better get something straight, cowboy,'' she told him as smoothly as if she meant it. ''In spite of what happened in the loft, I'm not looking for a tumble in the hay. Got that?''

Looking at her looking at him now, all wary and mad and wanting him in spite of herself, he could just imagine how good it would feel to pull that old scarf out of her hair and let it all loose, how fast she'd heat up once he put his hands on her.

But he wasn't going to. Not when something inside him felt as sore and tender as if he'd been stomped, had felt that way ever since he'd kissed her, and he didn't understand. He just knew he needed space, needed to move. ''Yeah,'' he said slowly, ''I think I've got it. Maybe you wouldn't mind, then, if I took you up on that offer you made a while back, and borrowed your truck. I'd like to head into town tonight for awhile.''

Those pretty lips thinned out. ''I'm sure you're feeling cooped up here.''

''Well, I'm surely not used to being without my truck. I thought I'd check out that bar on the edge of town. Papa Joe's. If,'' he added with a lift of his eyebrows, ''you don't object to my taking your truck there. I don't plan to tie one on or anything.''

''The Sundowner is a better place. Papa Joe's is pretty much a dive.''

He shrugged. ''Papa Joe's will have beer and pool and a jukebox…and maybe a little company.'' The company of a woman who was interested in a night's worth of mutual oblivion, a woman who didn't come with strings and price tags all over her.

Even though Chase had decided, while chasing a stubborn calf along Adams's fence line, that this was the best way to handle things, he didn't like the hurt that flickered in her eyes. He didn't like it at all.

Better, he told himself, to hurt her a little now, than a lot later.

"No problem," she said, and she was all dignity now. She turned, dismissing him, and started back toward the paddock where her students waited.

And dammit, he just couldn't leave it like that. "Summer."

Reluctantly, she paused and looked at him. The wind tossed her hair in her face. This time she ignored it.

"At least Raul didn't give the moldy hay to the horses," he pointed out. "I imagine that's what Fletcher wanted him to do. If he had, you'd have lost your horses, your income from lessons, every horse you board now, and you'd probably have ended up losing a good part of your kennel business, too, once word got out." She'd been sold out, yeah—and that was another reason for him to go into town tonight. But she hadn't been sold out completely.

He couldn't read her expression at all. "If you're right," she said at last, "I can't help wondering what Ray Fletcher will try next. If he was willing to use a teenage boy to try and kill my horses in order to drive me out of business, I'd say I've got a problem." And with that massive bit of understatement, she walked off.

Papa Joe's wasn't as dimly lit as some bars he'd been in, Chase reflected, but it probably should have been.

The smell of cigarette smoke and spilled beer was as

familiar to him as the Willie Nelson song playing on the jukebox. In his years on the circuit he must have been in a couple hundred places like this. Some played Willie, some played the Eagles, and a few played groups that sang in Spanish instead of English, but they were all pretty much the same.

Like the woman sitting next to him at the bar. She looked about the same to him as all the other women he'd passed a night or two with while on the road. They came in different shapes, shades and ages, yet they all looked alike.

This one was blond. "I'm gettin' dry, here, Chase," she said, jiggling the ice in her glass and turning slightly to give him a better view of what she had on display that night. They were nice breasts, firm and honey gold in a way that made it obvious she liked to sunbathe topless. She looked to be about twenty-two.

"Oh, I doubt that, sugar," he drawled, letting his gaze linger where she intended him to look. "You look pretty juicy to me."

She giggled. "My drink, you silly. I meant that my drink is about gone."

"Well, we'll have to do something about that, won't we..." He couldn't remember her name. Doris? Donna? What the hell was it? And why the hell couldn't he remember?

The itch hit him, the restless need to be elsewhere. Without questioning it, he gave the young woman with the nice breasts a slow smile and tossed a few bills on the bar. "Why don't you get us each another one, sugar, while I make a phone call, then join me over in the pool room. The table I paid for ought to be coming open pretty soon."

She pouted briefly to let him know he wasn't sup-

posed to play pool for too long. He winked at her and
walked away.

The pay phone was bolted to the back wall between
the men's and women's rest rooms. No privacy, but no
one paid any attention, either, as he dug out a fistful of
quarters and punched out a long distance number from
memory, a number he'd already called twice that evening.

"Mike?" he said when the male voice answered.
"How's the squirt?" He turned so his back was to the
wall—always a more comfortable position in a place
like this—and glanced around while he heard about the
piano recital his brother had just sat through.

Papa Joe's consisted of two rooms. This one held a
couple dozen matchbox-sized tables, a tiny dance floor,
the jukebox, bar and twenty-five or so men with less
than half that many women. The other room, reached
by passing through one of two arched doorways, held
six pool tables.

Raul wasn't there. Chase hadn't really expected him
to be, but it had been worth a chance. Raul had mentioned this place a couple times. Apparently Papa Joe
didn't mind renting a pool table or two to high school
kids, though he was too careful with his liquor license
to sell them anything else. Chase had hoped the kid
was stupid enough to show up tonight. With a little
encouragement, he figured he could at least get Raul to
confirm who had hired him.

So far, no luck.

Chase watched Doris-Delores wiggle her way towards the pool room, carrying his beer and her Tom
Collins.

Her jeans, and what she'd packed into them, drew
the eye of every man she passed. Chase knew he could

have her out of those jeans just as soon as he got her someplace private. He suspected he didn't have to be overly picky about the privacy, in fact.

So why didn't he care? He was about as excited over leaving here with Dora-with-the-nice-breasts as he would be over a case of alcohol-free beer.

"Give Jennifer a big hug from her Uncle Chase," he said to his brother, "and tell her she's double-wonderful, and I'm sorry I called too late to talk to her...yeah, that was me earlier. I didn't leave a message because I'm not where you can call me back...well, you're close. Ever heard of Papa Joe's, just outside San Antonio?"

They exchanged insults while Chase kept track of Darla's progress. It didn't matter, he told himself, if he wasn't exactly excited about Darlene. He'd respond just fine once he got to the interesting part. He needed something to settle his mind—something to keep him away from the wrong kind of woman. He didn't have to be enthusiastic. He hadn't gotten enthusiastic about much of anything since he woke up in that hospital in Las Vegas.

Except for a kiss in a stable. And the sight of a sunshine-bright woman in a big flannel shirt that showed damn little and made him want so much more.

Dammit all, he did not need this. He *was* going to get her out of his mind.

"The fact is," Chase said when Mike asked why he'd called, "I need a favor. Hell, no, not money. Would you shut up and listen? What I need is to get in touch with that broker you know in San Antonio, the one you met at...yeah, Gonzales. I need some information about a local land speculator, and I thought he might help me out. I'm trying to check out a situation here." He paused. Damn. Delilah had made it to the pool room finally, but some moron with a hairy chest and a beer gut was hassling her.

"Mmm—hmm," Chase said, scribbling a phone number on a scrap of paper. The moron had hold of Deanna's arm and was pulling on her, and she obviously didn't like it.

For the first time that night, Chase felt a prickle of real interest in something around him. "Sure, if you want to give him a call first so he'll be expecting me, that would be great," he said to his brother.

The moron pulled Dina into a one-armed embrace. She dumped the beer she'd been holding over his head. He bellowed.

"Uh, listen, Mike, I'd better go," Chase said as a second man grabbed the arm of the freshly christened ape, who let go of Donna and swung a fist at the other man. Chase hung up, grinning.

A fight. This was just what he needed to settle some of his frustrations, he thought happily as he started across the room.

"My God," Summer said, stopping dead in the doorway of the kennel the next morning at quarter to eight. She forgot about the math book in her hand, the reason she'd chased over here after Ricky, who always stopped by the kennel in the mornings now before school. "What happened to you?"

Chase met her gaze with as much dignity as a man can when his left eye is swollen up like a Halloween balloon—mostly black, with the yellow around the edges accented by interesting purplish streaks. "I ran into a door," he said, and bent stiffly to scoop dry dog food from the big silver trash can where it was stored.

Ricky giggled. "That's a joke, Mom."

"Yeah," Summer said dryly. She looked at Chase's damaged face and felt like her toes might leave the ground from relief. A horribly inappropriate relief. "I thought it might be."

"You didn't laugh," her son pointed out. Determined to help his battered hero, he, too, bent over the trash can to scoop out dog food. His head and one shoulder disappeared into the metal can, giving his voice a muffled echo when he said proudly, "It's one heck of a shiner, isn't it?"

"Oh, it's something, all right," Summer said. After the night she'd just spent, she didn't want to feel the least tug of sympathy for this man. Especially since it was certain to be all his own stupid, male fault he was hurting. But oh, my, that was one technicolor eye. "You can't even see out of it, can you?" she demanded, coming forward to join them. "Ricky, if you don't hurry you'll miss the bus."

"Ol' Mr. Perkins runs late all the time," he told her confidently, setting a filled dog food bowl on the floor and reaching for another empty one.

"Well, we aren't going to count on him running late, so move it. Here—" she said as he reluctantly started for the door. "You forgot your math book."

He made a face, but took the book. "I'll help you with the horses this afternoon, Chase," he called out as his legs started moving, automatically, at a faster and faster rate. He was out the door and out of sight by the time the next sentence floated back. "Bye, Mom!"

Summer smiled into the air after her departed son, then turned to look at her hired hand. Chase bent—slowly—to fill another bowl with kibble. Something about the way he wasn't looking at her reminded her of Ricky when her son had done something he should have known better than to do.

Her lips twitched in spite of herself. "You'd better let me have a look at your eye. I'm sure you didn't have the sense to get it checked last night."

"It's fine," he said shortly, still not looking her way.

When he straightened, she snatched the scoop out of his hand—something she would normally have been quite unable to do. Realizing this, she dropped the scoop and grabbed his hand.

He winced.

"I suppose you had to beat the heck out of the door," she said dryly, studying his swollen and battered knuckles, "for getting in your way." She let go of his hand. "Come on." She headed for the door.

"The dogs haven't been fed."

"They can wait a few minutes. The first aid kit I keep over here doesn't include a cold pack, and that's what your eye needs." She reached the door but didn't hear him following, so she glanced over her shoulder.

He still stood by the trash can, his mouth set in a line as stubbornly straight as his spine. "I told you that I'm fine."

Probably, she thought, it hurts less when he stands up extra straight that way. "You can't avoid feeling like an idiot," she pointed out, "when you've worked so hard at being one, even if I did let you refuse some basic first aid. Which I won't. Now come on."

He came.

This day was as sunny as the last one had been overcast. A meadowlark gurgled merrily in one of the three red oaks in front of the stable as Summer started across the yard. Subconsciously she imitated Ricky. Her legs moved faster and faster, as if she could outdistance the troubling echoes of the vast relief she'd felt upon first seeing Chase.

She felt so stupid this morning—stupid, and as light as if she'd swallowed helium. *Just because he got into a fight doesn't mean he didn't get into some other kind of trouble, too,* she reminded herself. It didn't say much for her maturity that she could be glad that some fool man went out and got himself stomped, now, did it? She knew better.

Chase caught up with her as she drew even with Horatio, who was munching on hay in the paddock. He held his old hat in one hand. "If we're racing," he drawled, "what do I get if I win?"

She sent one quick glance his way. Apparently he was over the attack of machismo that had made him reluctant to have her see his battered condition earlier. Now he looked entirely too pleased with himself. "I suppose I should be glad I didn't get a call from the sheriff last night," she said, "letting me know you were sleeping it off courtesy of the county."

"I didn't get drunk, and if anyone called the cops, it must have been after I left."

"So you brawl when you're stone-cold sober?"

His hand came up to feel gingerly around his swollen eye. "It seemed like a good idea at the time."

Summer had Chase sit at the kitchen table and hold the cold pack from the freezer to his face while she collected first aid supplies from the bathroom. When she saw her face in the mirrored medicine chest, the look in her eyes startled her.

Hope? What was there to hope for? So what if the blasted man *had* gotten into a fight instead of picking up a woman. It was just as possible he'd been fighting over the woman—or he'd had the fight and the woman both. Summer got the gauze, the peroxide and the tape, and stuck them into her sling. No, she was not about to start *hoping*. So what if he made her blood sing when he touched her, or when he smiled at her in that slow, lazy way he had?

Sex. That's all this feeling was, just sexual attraction, a mindless, instinctive drive she needn't feel any shame over. But she wasn't about to encourage it, either, or get it confused with any other sorts of feelings. Maybe he had held her close in the loft yesterday when she'd needed it. He'd flipped the switch from comfort to sex in a big hurry, hadn't he?

She was certainly not interested in a man like that. Summer nodded firmly to herself, grabbed the cotton balls, scissors and an antibacterial ointment, and went back to the kitchen—and stopped dead in the doorway.

He'd taken off his shirt.

His back was to the doorway where she stood staring, while his crossed arms rested on the back of the wooden chair. It was a splendid back, lean but tightly muscled. The strength and symmetry of him made her mouth go dry.

Somehow he knew she was there. He couldn't have heard the humming in her blood, or the way her heartbeat picked up, yet he looked over his shoulder and caught her gawking at him. And smiled, damn him. "As long as you're determined to play doctor," he said, "I thought you might as well have a look at this cut."

Sex, she reminded herself. Basic, mindless sex. That's all he was interested in, and it wasn't enough. "What cut?" she said as she got her legs moving, and added, "Put that cold pack back on your eye."

"It's more of a scratch, really. Here on my chest."

Well, that's where it would be, wouldn't it? she

thought, aggravated. "Turn your chair around, then, so I'll be able to get to it."

She sat catty-corner from him at the table, taking her time about setting her supplies out, putting off the moment when she looked at the cut—the one right there, on his chest—before she turned to face him.

Nice, she thought, dry-mouthed. *Very, very nice. Every bit as nice as his back.* Except for the nasty, four-inch-long cut slanting up from the top of his rib cage. "How did that happen?" She held the peroxide bottle in her left hand, uncapped it and managed to soak a cotton ball without dumping the peroxide all over. Her shoulder had improved enough to allow her some limited movement, thank goodness.

"Beer bottle." He winced slightly when she pressed the cotton ball to his wound. "After that, I decided things were getting messy, so I hunted up the door."

"I told you about that place." Stupid man. Maybe her fingers weren't as gentle as they might have been as she cleaned the dried blood off that very nice chest.

The edge of the cut crept up into the dusting of blond hair in the center, so her fingers had to follow it there. The hair was soft. Fuzzy. "Dammit," she said when he flinched, "hold still. Didn't I tell you that Papa Joe's is a dive? What did you go there for, anyway?" Now, that was a stupid question. He might just answer it.

He smiled. "Is this the part where you get to tell me what an idiot I was?"

She was not going to smile back. She knew better. Give a man like this one smile at the wrong time and he'd think—well, she wasn't sure what, except that it was bound to be wrongheaded. But with this irritating heat crawling under her skin, she was having a hard time remembering how she was supposed to act. "For heaven's sake, will you put that cold pack on your eye? It should take down the swelling."

"I doubt it'll help all that much today," he said, but he lifted the lumpy, blue gel pack and held it to his face. He watched her out of one amused eye as she squeezed the antibacterial ointment onto the fingertips of her right hand. "Now, if I'd had something cold to put on my eye last night it might have done some good, but I didn't think you'd like for me to wake you up in the middle of the night so you could tend my wounds."

Oh, but she'd been awake. Much as she'd hated herself for lying in bed listening for the sound of the truck, she'd done it. Much as she'd hated admitting it mattered whether her hired hand was with another woman that night, she'd done that, too, staring sleeplessly at her ceiling even after she'd heard the truck pull up into the yard.

She set the tube down, reached out and smoothed the ointment on carefully. And yawned.

His eyebrows went up. "Tired this morning?"

"No." *Good one, Summer. He's really going to believe that.* "A little." Her fingertips tingled as she spread the salve over his cut. "I'm afraid I let myself worry a bit last night. Do you really think someone wants to drive me out of business?"

The teasing vanished from his face and voice. "I don't know." He paused. "I didn't see Raul last night."

"Did you expect to?"

"He plays pool at Papa Joe's sometimes. I wanted to ask him some questions. And no," he said steadily, watching her face as he set down the gel pack, "that wasn't the main reason I went there last night."

She didn't want to ask. The fact that she didn't want

to know, that some cowardly corner of her preferred ignorance to truth, tightened her lips. She squeezed more ointment onto her fingers. "Give me your hand. Your right one. It's the worst."

Wordlessly he laid his hand on the corner of the table.

She smoothed the white cream over the place where the skin was split across one knuckle. "So why did you go there, Chase?"

"To get lucky."

Her fingers froze—then, slowly, went on to the next knuckle. She didn't look up. "Is there some reason you thought I should know that?"

"Yeah. Because it's your fault I didn't."

That brought her head up, her eyes narrowing in anger. "Jimmie used to say that. If he partied too much it was my fault because I made him feel tied down, and that made him crazy. If he didn't party at all, that was my fault, too, because I made him feel too guilty to enjoy himself."

"I'm not Jimmie, and that wasn't what I meant. Here." Slowly he withdrew his right hand and held his left one out for her to tend. "I meant that it didn't feel right to be with another woman when all I could think about was you." Although one corner of his mouth turned up, his eyes weren't smiling at all. "I got into the fight because that seemed easier than figuring out why I didn't want the pretty young thing I'd met. She should have been just what I was looking for."

"So what was it you were looking for?" Summer kept her voice a good deal steadier than her insides as she squeezed out more ointment. "Someone who'd fall into your bed nice and easy, then climb out again with no complaints when the time came for you to move on?''

"Yeah," he said, the half smile hooked on his lips as if he'd forgotten it was there. "That's pretty much what I thought I was there for, all right. Which makes me sound like a pretty sorry son of a gun to you, doesn't it? Of course, it turned out I was wrong."

"It makes you sound like most rodeo cowboys I've known," she said. "Out for a good time before you move on down the road. Not that it's any of my business." She didn't look up. It took all her concentration to keep her hand steady as she stroked the salve into his knuckles.

"I don't think it's helping."

Her eyes flew to his face. Her fingers paused.

"To take down the swelling," he said softly, pulling his hand away from hers. "I don't think the swelling is going down at all."

Her pulse rate sure wasn't going down. No, the look in his eyes kicked it up from a canter to a full gallop. "You didn't give it enough time."

"I'm not feeling patient." He raised both bruised hands to her face and cupped it. The gesture was one of control rather than tenderness. He held her still, staring at her for three beats of her heart—just long enough that she knew, they both knew, she could have protested what he was about to do.

But she didn't.

He didn't kiss her mouth. His lips went to first one cheek, then the other. Trailed up over an eyelid, then slowly down along her jaw, and her heart did a scared little dance while the heat built in her blood. When his mouth moved to her throat she tilted her head to give him better access, and the flick of his tongue made her think about having his mouth on her breasts. When his mouth moved back up to tease hers she shifted in her chair, wanting him to move one of his hands from her face to the place where she ached for him.

The power of that longing jerked her out of his hold, much the way an explosion can put out a fire by robbing it of oxygen. For a moment she couldn't get her breath, as if the blast he'd set off inside her had indeed stolen her air. "No," she said at last, as much to herself as to him. "No, I don't want this."

"I don't suppose it matters much whether you want it to happen or not," he said, unwinding his long body from the chair and looking down at her with no smile at all on his face. "Sooner or later we'll be lovers, Summer."

"I'm not one of your easy come, easy go women." She felt each throb of her heart as passion and panic combined to thicken her blood.

"No, you damn sure aren't, are you? You're no more what I ought to want than I'm what you should want, but in the end it isn't going to matter. The only way you can keep me from having you, Summer, is to get rid of me. Fire me. Now. Are you going to do that?"

She looked at him and said nothing.

"I didn't think so," he said softly. "I'll give you a little time, boss lady, to get used to the idea. But not much." He grabbed his shirt from the back of his chair and his hat from the table.

Summer didn't watch as Chase walked out the door. She stared straight ahead when the wooden *thunk* of the door closing told her he was gone. She sat there and waited for the debris from that earlier explosion to start settling, so maybe her brain could start working again.

But for several long minutes, all she could think was that this was one hell of a time to realize she was beginning to fall for Chase McGuire.

Six

___

Summer didn't intend to go down without a fight.

By afternoon of the next day, clouds had drawn another gray veil across the sky, and a fine rain kept everything slick and wet. Summer had several errands to do in town that day, including getting the word out that she needed another part-time hand.

Sure, she was avoiding Chase again. He was bound to realize it, too—especially since she arranged her errands so she'd be gone at lunch. She left him something to eat on the table, along with a note asking him to keep the cordless phone with him and take messages. So she was being pretty obvious about her need to stay away from him. But after the way she'd acted when he kissed her, being obvious was the least of her worries.

She had a lot to think about, and she couldn't get any of it straight in her mind if he was nearby.

How hard can it be, she asked herself as she pulled

up in Maud's driveway that afternoon at two, *to avoid falling for a man who's no more likely to stay in one place than the wind?* It didn't matter if he was the sexiest thing she'd ever seen in jeans, or that she'd learned there were things she could like about him and even admire. Surely she couldn't fall in love with a man like him—a wanderer, a man unlikely to ever be satisfied with a single place or a single woman.

Yet she hadn't fired him.

Maud opened the door before the echo from the doorbell had completely died away.

"I thought I'd see if I could talk you into giving me a cup of coffee," Summer said, knowing she was about to be obvious again and delight her meddlesome friend. "And we never finished our talk the other day, did we? The one where you were going to tell me how Chase hurt his knee."

Maud's wrinkled face lit up. "Well, come in, then! Come on back to the kitchen," she ordered, bustling through her immaculate living room with its doilies and polished cherry tables, "while I put the coffee on, and we'll have a nice talk."

Summer followed her to the small, green-and-white kitchen at the back of the house, knowing she'd let herself in for a major inquisition. But she had to know more about Chase.

"So," Maud said as she sat down at the kitchen table opposite Summer, while coffee perked in her old metal pot. "Are you ready to admit you're interested in that good-looking hired hand of yours? He does have a nice butt, doesn't he?"

Summer shook her head, amused at her old friend, who was pink with pleasure at her own audacity. "It would be foolish of me to be interested. He's not a man who'll stay.''

"You can't be sure of that," Maud said stubbornly. "He gave up rodeoing, didn't he? Maybe he's just drifting now because he doesn't know what to do with himself. Maybe a good woman could give him some ideas about that. I think he's worth taking a chance on.''

But Summer didn't want a chancy sort of a man. She didn't want a man at all. She wanted guarantees, and there weren't any, not when it came to men...even the ones who seemed safe. And *safe* was the last word she'd use to describe Chase McGuire. "I'm not much of a risk taker anymore, Maud. Is that coffee ready?"

By the time Summer had drunk a cup of Maud's muddy coffee, she knew everything the old woman knew about Chase's accident. He'd drawn a real rogue for his first ride in the bareback competition at the NFR fifteen months ago, and he'd been thrown. One of the horse's hooves had clipped his head on the way down, knocking him silly. The horse had turned on his downed rider, and Chase had ended up in the hospital with a couple of cracked ribs, a minor concussion...and a shattered kneecap.

"At least he had the sense to get out," Maud said. "Of rodeo, I mean. You see some of those cowboys keep at it year after year no matter how banged up they get. You want some more coffee?"

"No, thanks." Summer frowned. How bad was Chase's knee? It seemed—oh, odd, out of character, for him to have dropped out of rodeo so completely, unless his knee was worse than she'd realized. Pain by itself wasn't enough to make a rodeo cowboy leave the circuit, any more than pain stopped a quarterback or a world-class gymnast from competing.

Was Chase's knee so weak he couldn't keep his legs around a bronc tightly enough to make it to the buzzer? "I'd better get back to the house. Ricky will be home from school in another twenty minutes."

The phone rang. "Hang on a minute," Maud said as she went to answer it.

Since the phone was on the kitchen wall, Summer could see right away by Maud's expression the news wasn't good. "You'd better talk to her yourself," Maud said to the caller. "She's right here, Rosie." She held the phone out.

Summer listened to Rosie in silence the first few minutes, disbelief and anger warring for top billing. "But I've lived here all my life! People here know me!" Or she had thought they did. "How could anyone believe that about me?" Rosie's assurances that she didn't believe the story for a minute helped a little. Just a little, since obviously some people did believe it. "I'd like to know who started it. A rumor this vicious is going to affect more than my feelings. My business…yes, I understand your position, Rosie," Summer said finally, "but I don't have to like it."

Summer hung up the phone. If she'd had any lingering doubts about whether someone was trying to drive her out of business, she didn't anymore. "Mind if I make a couple more calls, Maud?" she asked grimly.

Ten minutes later Summer stood at Maud's front door, taking her leave.

"Remember that you've got friends," the old woman said, patting her arm reassuringly. "You're not in this alone."

"I'll remember." Impulsively Summer bent down to give the tiny woman a hug. "With you on my side I figure I'm halfway in the clear already. I know I can count on you.''

"Of course you can,'' Maud said gruffly, returning the hug, then stepping back to fix Summer with a no-nonsense look. "There's something else you should remember. You talked about taking risks earlier. Doing nothing is taking a risk, too. Sometimes it's the biggest risk of all.''

"Chase?'' Ricky asked. "Is something wrong?''

They stood in the stable next to the tack room. Chase had been cleaning the stalls on the north side, whose occupants were currently in the pasture. Ricky had just arrived and started helping when the phone rang a couple of minutes ago.

Some evidence remained of Chase's stupidity at Papa Joe's the night before. His eye was still colorful, though it was more green and yellow than purple-black now, and his scabbed-over knuckles looked bad, but the day's work had loosened him up some. But it wasn't his aches that had Chase frowning as he ended the call.

Summer wasn't back.

Chase smoothed his expression, hooking the cordless phone on his belt. "Just some business stuff your mother will need to know about,'' he said easily. Summer would have to decide what to tell Ricky about the phone call Chase had just taken from the owner of one of the horses she boarded.

He'd taken a couple of other calls since lunch—one had been from Rosie, who'd wanted Summer to call her the minute she got back. The other, about twenty minutes ago, had been from Summer. She'd told him only that she'd already talked to Rosie, that something had come up, and would he mind keeping an eye on Ricky until she got home?

Something was definitely wrong, but Chase didn't have much more of an idea what it might be than Ricky did. He picked up the spring tooth rake. He'd already shoveled up the manure from all ten stalls, and now had to remove the damp straw and shavings and rake the packed earth floor.

"I guess maybe you could use some help mucking out, with Raul gone and all," Ricky said, standing with his thumbs stuck, cowboy-style, in his belt loops. "I could dump the manure and bedding. Mom has me do that sometimes. I won't even charge you for it. Unless, of course, you just *want* to pay me."

Chase shot him an amused glance. "You needing money for something, Rick?"

The boy's mouth, as mobile as his mother's, stretched in a wide grimace. "Mom's birthday is next month and I'm saving up to get her some of this perfume from the drugstore. Moms like that sort of thing, you know."

"So I've heard." Summer's birthday was next month, was it? Chase considered that as he worked, wondering if he'd still be here. Was it at the end of the month, or the beginning? "I guess we could work something out."

Ricky made several trips to the wide, shallow hole where Summer composted the manure and soiled straw, and he helped Chase lime the wet spots in the stalls, chattering a mile a minute the whole time. That didn't bother Chase. The boy was obviously hungry for male companionship, and Chase didn't mind obliging him. Actually, having Ricky hang around felt good. Real good.

Chase had always enjoyed the youngsters at rodeos, and he was crazy about his niece, but this was the first time he'd been around a kid day after day like this. If he'd ever thought about it, he would have expected he'd get tired of the boy's company after a while. Somehow it hadn't happened that way.

The sun was a hidden glow near the western edge of the world, and Chase and Ricky had started moving the horses in from pasture, when Summer's car pulled up. Ricky took off running. Chase followed more slowly, and not just because of the lingering stiffness from last night.

He wasn't looking forward to telling Summer about the phone calls.

Summer parked her little blue car next to the house. Ricky reached the car at the same moment she swung open the door. He was yammering a mile a minute about school and a Scout meeting that night, and some kind of cookies he was supposed to take. From halfway across the yard Chase could see her wince. "Oh, Lord, I forgot the meeting. Don't worry, champ," she said, ruffling his hair. "I'll stir something up. I brought home pizza, so there's time."

"Pizza!" Ricky dived into the car for the box.

She looked tired, Chase thought. Tired and pale. "What's wrong?" he asked as he reached them.

"Wrong?" She ran a hand over her hair, which hung loose, and glanced at her son as he crawled backward out of the car with the pizza box. "All sorts of things. Taxes keep going up, and the Middle East is a mess." She grimaced. "So am I, but it'll keep until after supper."

She didn't want to talk about it in front of Ricky. He

understood, but he needed to tell her about one caller, at least. "The phone's been busy."

Her eyes locked with his for a second. He saw frustration and anger clouding those summer-sky eyes. "Take the pizza on in the house, please, Rick," she said. "Put it on the table, wash up and pour us all something to drink."

"Coke?" he asked eagerly.

She smiled. "Yeah, we can have Coke. Go on, now. Chase and I need to talk business a minute."

For once Ricky didn't run. Pizza was, apparently, too important to take any chances with. Chase didn't realize he was watching the boy, grinning over his careful progress to the back door, until Summer's bleak voice recalled his attention.

"So what have you heard?"

He gave it to her straight. "Rhonda Patterson called to say that she's behind you all the way, but she didn't say about what. Jim Hughes wants you to call him. Sharon Estes is coming by to get her mare. Tonight. And she expects you to refund her the rest of the month's board."

Summer said a few choice words under her breath.

His eyebrows went up. "I think you owe the penalty box about five bucks on that one." Chase had heard from Ricky about that penalty box.

She didn't smile. "Did she say why?"

"Not exactly."

"What did she say?"

"Something about where there's smoke there's fire, and she's had her doubts ever since you got hooked up with that 'rodeo bum.' Apparently she's one of those who thinks rodeo is cruel to animals." He hesitated. "If she was talking about me—"

"She was talking about Jimmie. And you're right. Nothing has ever convinced Sharon that good bucking horses are treated better than her precious Ginger, whose teeth are going to rot, since she insists on feeding the poor thing sugar all the time. But this—her current problem—has nothing to do with Jimmie or you or the rodeo. Just me."

Chase had no idea he was angry until he heard himself demand, "So what the hell is going on?"

Instead of answering she turned around, opened the car and took something from the glove compartment. It was a folded-up newspaper, or part of one. "Here," she said wearily. "This will explain. I've got to go in and get started on those cookies." She turned and headed for the kitchen.

The day slid from evening into twilight, cloud cover robbing it of any touch of sunset's warmth, while Chase read the article. He didn't curse or throw the paper down or rip it up. His anger was too cold and slow to be satisfied that way. It bothered him, that anger. It wasn't what he was used to.

Stripped of frills, the story said that someone had filed a complaint two weeks ago with the president of the local SPCA, claiming that Summer mistreated her own animals and neglected those in her care. The president—Jim Hughes, the man who'd called for her earlier—had dismissed the complaint as completely unfounded, saying that such accusations were absurd to anyone who knew Summer. But the anonymous complainant hadn't let it drop. He or she had contacted the local weekly paper, accusing the president of hushing things up because of Summer's position on the SPCA board.

Ray Fletcher. An image of that deceptively soft-looking man with a lizard's cold, quick eyes formed in Chase's mind. Somehow the developer was behind this.

Chase looked over at the cheerful little frame house where his supper of takeout pizza waited. The curtains at the kitchen window were open, as usual. He could see Summer moving around, getting out ingredients for the cookies, laughing, listening, putting on a great show so Ricky wouldn't worry.

Fletcher wasn't going to get away with this, he promised himself and her. There was no way, no way in heaven or hell, that Chase was going to let that piece of scum get away with blackening Summer's name, much less stealing her land.

He just didn't know how a broken-down rodeo cowboy was going to stop the man.

Somehow Summer finished the cookies in time. She even managed to eat a slice of pizza, partly because when Chase came in he made such a big deal about her skipping meals. The way the man acted, you'd think he knew she'd been so busy avoiding him she'd missed lunch, but he couldn't, of course.

Yet he knew other things he shouldn't have known. He didn't ask her one question about that damned article, because he knew she didn't want to talk about it in front of Ricky. He didn't ask any other questions, either, not the doubting sort of questions she'd braced herself to see in his eyes after handing him that newspaper. People she'd known her whole life might be wondering about her now, but Chase wasn't.

That sort of thing could shake any woman up.

By the time Summer took the last cookie sheet out of the oven, Chase had eaten and left. He had to finish bringing in the horses and give them their grain, a chore that had been Raul's in the past, and one that Summer had meant to take care of herself.

Summer and Ricky were just leaving, gingerbread cookies still warm in their plastic carrier, when Sharon Estes pulled up outside the gate in her shiny Ford pickup, horse trailer in tow. Summer stopped with her hand on the car door. "Go on and get in, Ricky," she said, her temper sparking. "And don't eat any more of those cookies. I'll be right back."

"What does Ms. Estes want, Mom?"

Chase stepped out of the shadows near the stable. "I'll take care of it."

She scowled. "You most certainly will not."

The big light under the stable's eaves showed her his expression clearly as he crossed the thirty feet between the stable and Summer's car. He looked...different. More dangerous somehow, and it wasn't just the disreputable effect of that fading shiner.

She thought suddenly of a bow and arrow, and the graceful motion of an archer drawing his bow, deceptively smooth and easy. Smooth and easy—just like Chase McGuire. She shivered.

He stopped a few steps away. "Well, now, I understand why you'd rather deal with her yourself," he said. "After all, I can't hit her. She's a woman," he pointed out in his lazy drawl. "But it's still better if I talk to her. I can't help thinking it might look unprofessional if you punch her out. Can't say that I blame you for wanting to, but it won't help. Trust me on that."

"Are you mad at Ms. Estes, Mom?" Ricky asked, excited. "Are you going to—"

"No, I am not going to punch her," she said, exasperated. She looked at Ricky. She wasn't going to be able to keep all this from him, was she? Her anger went up another notch. "And yes, I am mad at Ms. Estes. Someone said some rotten things about how I treat my animals, and she believed them."

"Well, that sucks!"

Her mouth twitched. "Yeah, it does."

"You and Ricky are going to be late for that meeting," Chase said as Sharon Estes teetered toward the big gate in her high heels and snug skirt. Obviously, the woman had rushed out here to rescue her horse from Summer's clutches without even changing clothes after getting off work at the Days Ease Inn.

Summer's lips thinned. She opened her car door because Chase was right. If she dealt with Sharon herself, she was going to lose her temper.

"Go on," he said softly when she still hesitated. "You don't want to end up apologizing."

"Tell her not to come back. I don't want her business. And she's not getting any damned refund."

"I'll tell her. I'll keep an eye on her, too. Make sure she only gets her own stuff."

Oh, that would go over well. Sharon went to church twice a week and had an irritating tendency to offer to pray for people who didn't. Summer grinned suddenly. "Good idea," she said, and climbed into the car. "Chase?"

"Yeah?"

"Thanks." It wasn't as hard to say as she would have thought.

"Anytime."

No, she thought as she drove off. Not "anytime," because in another six or seven weeks he'd be gone. It was a good thing she knew that. Otherwise, the blasted man might have undone her completely just now. She'd never known how seductive unquestioning support and understanding could be.

Between the Scout meeting and Ricky's bath and bedtime story, Summer stayed busy until after nine o'clock. As usual, Ricky fell asleep almost the minute she shut off his light.

Ten minutes later Summer stood in her quiet living room listening to the ticking of the clock on the bookcase. Her father had put her in charge of winding the old Seth Thomas mantel clock when she was four. To teach her responsibility, he'd said. The sound of it now was as comforting as the rhythm of a loved one's heartbeat. Summer moved to the clock, took the key from its hiding place on the back and automatically began winding the clock.

While she turned the key, she thought about the newspaper article. She thought about staying inside her cozy living room, and she thought about risk.

Summer put the key back where it belonged. Carefully she removed the sling that she wore throughout the day to keep her arm immobile and laid it on the back of the couch. Then she walked out of the living room, down the short hall to the darkened kitchen. The back door creaked when she opened it. She stepped onto the porch, her own, familiar back porch. The chilly air was thick with darkness and risk.

"Rick asleep?"

The low voice from the end of the porch didn't startle her. She hadn't seen him, but she hadn't needed to. She'd known he was there. Waiting. "Yes. He always goes out like a light once he stops moving long enough."

"I've noticed."

Yes, he'd stayed around after supper enough nights to have noticed that sort of thing, hadn't he? Playing checkers or Chutes and Ladders with Ricky, or watching a sitcom before heading back to his narrow bed at the kennel. It was odd behavior for a determined roamer.

She'd worried about Chase's effect on her son, but he'd been good for Ricky, rubbing some of the glitter off Ricky's idea of what the rodeo was like, teaching him important lessons by example about work and humor and the difference between a man's confidence and a boy's bragging.

Summer started toward Chase, holding her left arm carefully close to her body. Her eyes were already pretty well adjusted to the darkness, and she could see him at the north end of the porch, leaning against the railing—a lean black shape against the grayer darkness around him. When he straightened suddenly, she saw the motion as a blurring of darknesses. "Fletcher is behind this."

"Probably." She was amazed by how cool her voice sounded when her heart was pounding so hard. "I talked to Jim Hughes, the SPCA president, this afternoon, but he couldn't tell me anything except that I have his support. So I went to see the editor of the paper, who is also the only reporter. He told me one of my neighbors brought the complaint."

"Damn." Vaguely she could tell that he moved again, this time so that he faced her. She caught the faint gleam of his eyes. "Fletcher probably bribed someone. Do you have any idea who it might be?"

"I think so, but I can't be sure." She stopped in front of him. Close enough to feel the warmth of him only a foot away. She inhaled slowly, carefully, so he wouldn't hear, drawing his scent in—the smell of dirt and horses and man, a hint of sweat, and some faint, private note that was Chase. Only Chase.

"Well? Who do you think it was?"

She shook her head.

"You don't have to worry," he said dryly. "If I haven't taken a tire iron after Fletcher yet, I can probably restrain myself with your anonymous neighbor, too."

She felt her pulse in her throat, in her chest and lower, between her legs. "Did you want to, then?" she asked, and her voice wasn't quite so cool anymore.

"I'm not going to let him get away with this."

"How are you going to stop him?" She didn't like the sharpness in her voice. She liked the fear that lay behind it even less. She ran a hand over her hair, finger combing it back out of her face. She hadn't stopped to brush it before coming out here, afraid that if she did, she'd lose her nerve and stay in her safe, quiet living room. "I didn't mean it like that. I just don't know what to do."

"It's a perfectly good question." For the first time since she came out here, she heard some of his usual humor in his voice. "I don't know how to stop him, not yet. But I've got an appointment tomorrow with a man named Henry Gonzales in San Antonio. He's...I guess you'd call him a money man. My brother has dealt with him some, and Gonzales considers himself obligated to Mike for something Mike told him once. I'm hoping he'll agree to give us some information about Fletcher. If we knew why Fletcher wants your land so badly it might help."

Summer was surprised into silence. She'd heard of Henry Gonzales. He had a finger in half the pies in the San Antonio area. That Chase's brother knew the man, had dealt with him enough that Chase hoped to trade on the association, disoriented her. Softly she said, "I really don't know much about you, do I?"

Silence hung between them for a moment, a silence as taut as the bow she'd thought of earlier, a bow drawn tight and ready. Then Chase's answer drifted across the blindness of night that lay between them. "What more do you need to know? My age? Thirty-one. My favorite color? Blue. Summer-sky blue."

He moved closer, a solid, warm shape in the darkness, a force she could feel all along her. His hands settled on her shoulders. His voice was low, private. "You aren't wearing your sling, Summer. Why did you take it off?"

She could have lied. She didn't want to. The truth stuck in her throat along with the speeding beat of her heart.

Carefully, irresistibly, he eased her up to him. "Maybe there are other things you need to know about me. Like how my hands feel against your bare skin," he murmured. "Or you might want to learn what I like to do in the dark. Shall I show you what I like, Summer?"

Her thighs were inches from his. Her left arm was trapped gently between them, keeping her breasts from touching his chest. She ached with a hunger as slow and lazy and hot as an afternoon in July. "You aren't going to seduce me, Chase," she said, lifting her good arm to wrap it around his neck.

"No?" His head bent, slowly. His lips skimmed hers, once.

"Nope." She opened her mouth and gently, firmly, bit his bottom lip. His body was so close she felt the jolt that went through him. "You can't seduce a willing woman. But—"

The rest of what she would have said was lost in the sweetness of his mouth taking hers. He tasted like the dreams she'd pretended so hard she didn't dream anymore. He tasted like danger and hunger and choices so huge she couldn't even guess how much she hazarded by coming willfully, eagerly, into his arms—wonderful arms, warm and solid, one at her waist, one lower, at her hips. He was careful, this time, of her arm trapped between them.

She didn't want to be careful. She wanted her arm out of the way and her sweater, too. She wanted light, not darkness, so she could see if he really liked her breasts. And when his big hand spread over her bottom and his leg moved between hers, his thigh pressing upward into her center, she wanted a great deal more.

Summer moaned. Chase trembled, and hoped she didn't know. There in the secret darkness on the back porch, he slid his hand beneath her sweater. He refused to hurry. He wanted this too much to take any chance of frightening her now. First he savored the soft skin of her back, the dip of her spine. Then, slowly, he brought his hand around to her front.

The muscles of her stomach jumped when he stroked her there. Her breath caught. The roar of his blood nearly deafened him as he moved his hand up and covered her breast firmly.

Her nipple was hard against his palm. It needed attention, he knew, needed pressure and touching and tonguing, but for some reason he couldn't move, could only stand there, caught by this moment when he held Summer's naked breast and kissed her slowly, slowly, his mouth tender and greedy.

When she moved her head just enough to break the contact between their mouths, he didn't protest. He bent to kiss her neck instead, where secret hollows trapped her scent.

"Chase…"

"Mmm." At last he made his hand move, releasing the warm weight of her breast long enough to catch her nipple between his thumb and fingers. He rubbed it.

Her low moan delighted him. So did the way she moved against his thigh. "Chase, there's something I need to say. I—oh, heavens. You have to stop for a minute. I can't think."

He didn't want her to think. He wanted to lower her to the hard, wooden floor of the porch, pull her jeans and panties down and bury himself in her. Quickly, before she thought about what she was doing. His hand dropped to the waistband of her jeans. He undid the button.

She said his name again, breathless, plaintive—and if that was a plea for him to stop, it was a plea he could ignore. She was too far gone, lost in the needs of her body, and he knew that he could unzip her jeans and put his hand inside, he could touch her where she needed to be touched, and he could have her. Here, on the porch, with the night draped around them for privacy.

He didn't know why he stopped.

She stood with her face pressed into his shoulder. His hand was spread across her belly on the outside of her jeans, his fingertips touching the soft swell of her mound. Her breath was as ragged as his.

"You warned me," she said after a moment, her voice low and husky. "I think I owe it to you to warn you, too."

He had no idea what she was talking about.

"You told me we would be lovers, that you weren't going to wait long." Now she straightened her head, looking straight at him. Her skin was a pale blur in the darkness. The liquid surface of her eyes caught some vagrant gleam from the light by the stable or the shrouded moon. "So I'm telling you my intentions. They're…not the same as yours. I don't want to be a temporary lover."

Something dark fluttered at the edges of his mind like bat wings in the blackness. "I won't stay," he told her, and he took his hands away from her. In spite of the way his body ached and craved, he let her go. "Don't fool yourself into thinking differently."

"I intend to do everything I can to change your mind."

It wasn't his mind that needed changing—it was fate, life, the universe. He *couldn't* stop moving on down the road. He stepped back. It wasn't what he decided to do, wasn't even what he wanted to do. "Well, honey, I guess you've done what you set out to do, then. I've changed my mind. I don't want you all that much, after all."

He heard the quick catch of her breath and wondered, distantly, if she was going to hit him again. Or cry.

He wasn't prepared for what she did do.

Her hand reached unerringly across the darkness between them. She curled her fingers around him where he was hot, hard, and throbbing beneath the denim, and he froze in shock and pleasure so intense he couldn't breathe. She squeezed him once and let go.

Then she turned and walked away, but he heard her taunt as clearly as if she'd spoken it aloud: *Liar.*

Seven

"Come right this way, Mr. McGuire, Ms. Callaway. Mr. Gonzales is expecting you."

Chase stood and waited politely, so Summer had no choice but to walk in front of him. She felt self-conscious in her second-best dress, a plain yellow sheath with a boxy jacket that she'd liked pretty well until she had to wear it to ask a favor of a multimillionaire. The ugly blue sling she wore with it didn't help.

Neither the secretary nor the reception area were what she'd expected of a man who'd made a fortune wheeling and dealing in real estate, cattle and whatever else took his interest. His secretary was frumpy, with thick bifocals and a voice as liquid as the wind sieving through the leaves on an oak tree. Dimestore dreck like the red plastic egg crate sat next to museum-quality antiques in the cluttered reception area.

Summer led the way into Henry Gonzales's office, uncomfortably conscious of the man behind her, and tried not to let her hips sway too much.

The man behind the untidy desk stood when Summer entered. Henry Gonzales was short—several inches shorter than her—with a thick, black mustache, thinning black hair combed in careful strands across his bald spot, a wrinkled shirt and a pot belly. "Señora," he said, "please come in and bless my eyes with your beauty."

Summer smiled tentatively, feeling more comfortable. She was familiar with the Latin fondness for compliments, but she'd seldom heard one expressed with such charming formality. *"Gracias, Señor Gonzales. Y gracias por su tiempo este día."*

He beamed at her and launched into a burst of rapid-fire Spanish.

She shook her head as she sat in one of the two chairs facing him. "I'm afraid my Spanish isn't that good. I only know a little bit."

"And my Spanish is even worse, since I don't know any," Chase said, folding his lean body into the chair next to hers. "At least, none I can use around a lady."

Summer didn't look at him. She'd been doing her best not to look at Chase ever since he came to her door at lunch to ask her for the keys to her truck so he could keep his appointment with Henry Gonzales. She'd insisted on going with him, of course, but that didn't mean she had to *look* at him.

It had not been a comfortable ride into the city.

"Ah, then we will stay with the English," Gonzales said, and turned to Chase. "It is good to meet you, Mr. McGuire. I have heard much about you from your excellent brother, and, as I told him, I will be glad to lend you some small assistance. I hope he is well? And your beautiful little niece? I believe that, unlike my Rose, she faces another operation still, does she not?''

Operation? Summer's curiosity overcame her embarrassment. She glanced at the man seated next to her.

He leaned back in his chair, one leg crossed over the other man-style, his right ankle resting on left knee. Today Chase looked every inch a rodeo cowboy. A bit gaudy. Flamboyant. Willing, unlike most males these days, to flaunt his plumage a bit. In addition to his black Stetson with the concha band, Chase wore a hot pink Western shirt, a tooled leather belt with an engraved silver buckle and black boots that had probably cost as much as an untrained yearling. "That's right," he said. "She's got one more facing her still next year."

"La pobrecita," Gonzales said, shaking his head. "So many operations, and therapy is difficult, is it not? But what can be done with medical technology today is little short of a miracle, and one for which I thank God daily. An expensive miracle, of course. Little Jennifer is lucky to have an uncle who made so much money in the rodeo. Mayhew Clinic provides the best, but the best is costly."

A little girl who needed a lot of operations? An uncle who made a lot of money in the rodeo—and was flat broke now? Summer stared at Chase.

He shifted uneasily in his chair. "They're the best, all right. I hear from Mike that they worked some pretty great magic for your Rose. Ballet, I think he said?"

"I have pictures," Gonzales said, beaming again. "Before you leave I will make you look at some. But now, I suppose, we should discuss what brings you to me today."

Summer let Chase do the talking. This was his idea,

and if Henry Gonzales did decide to help them with some information about Ray Fletcher, it would be because of Chase and his brother…and his little niece, who was fortunate to have an uncle who made so much money in the rodeo.

"So," Gonzales said crisply when Chase finished describing recent events at Three Oaks, "you have suspicions. Cause is easier to believe in than coincidence, yes? However, the business world may have its sharks, but it would be odd for a successful developer to risk so much for a scrap of land, however valuable to his plans. It is a matter of the profit-to-risk ratio, you understand? Still, it is not impossible."

"Can you help us find out which it is—cause or coincidence?" Chase asked bluntly.

"I will gather a little information and get back to you. In the meantime I advise you to be careful of what you say outside of this room."

He turned to Summer. "If Mr. McGuire *is* right about Fletcher being behind your recent misfortunes, the man would be pleased to have an opportunity to sue for slander, you see. Such a suit might be impossible to win, but I think you do not have the resources to fight it properly, Señora Callaway, is that right?"

Summer nodded stiffly.

"And it would be a further drain, both emotionally and financially. However, you might want to tell people that it is ridiculous to suppose Mr. Fletcher could be behind such harassment. You understand? You give people the idea by denying it."

Summer smiled. She liked that notion.

"Now I must ask you a few questions about the property and about Fletcher's original proposal to purchase it."

She reached for the oversize purse she'd brought. "I brought a copy of the legal description of the land, if that helps. It's the survey that was included when my father took out a mortgage on it several years ago."

"Excellent. But tell me—is this mortgage still in place?"

"Yes, but I've paid it way down. And Mr. Newberry, my banker, would never sell the loan to Fletcher," she assured him. John Newberry had known her all her life.

Gonzales went on to ask many more questions—about mineral rights, school zones and the board at Bita Creek's only bank. And before they left, he did pull out a handful of photos of a pretty young girl wearing a crown of shiny black braids and a white satin tutu. Summer learned that the little girl had been injured in an auto accident three years ago, and there had been some doubt as to whether she would walk again. But now here she was, dancing! A miracle that belonged in equal parts, Gonzales said, to his daughter's determination and to the skill of the surgeons at Mayhew Clinic—the place Chase's brother had told Henry Gonzales about.

Outside, Chase asked her if she had any other errands she needed to take care of before they headed back. She thanked him politely and said no. He held the pickup door for her before climbing into the driver's seat. Neither of them spoke.

San Antonio traffic was always heavy. Summer didn't like driving in the city. She never had, and saw no point in insisting on taking the wheel just to prove she could. She had other things to think about, like whether or not Ray Fletcher was trying to drive her out of business so she'd be forced to sell him her land, and what she could do about it if he was. In a way it would be a relief to find out Fletcher was behind some of her problems. It was easier to accept having a human enemy than to think that God or fate was out to get her.

Then there was the question of what on earth she was supposed to say to the man she'd groped last night in the darkness.

Summer's face heated when she thought of that, just as it had been doing off and on all day. Lord, she couldn't believe she'd done that. Even in the wild days of her youth she'd never done anything quite so... obvious.

She had a vivid tactile memory of exactly what Chase felt like through the worn denim of his jeans. She tried not to dwell on it.

"Have you had any luck finding another hand?" Chase asked abruptly as he pulled into the heavy traffic on I-10.

For a second Summer sat there and blinked stupidly at the cars around them. "Another hand?"

"To replace Raul." Chase threaded the truck through the traffic skillfully.

"Oh. No, not yet," she said, her heartbeat not yet recovered. "I've put the word out, and I expect I'll find someone soon. I know it's a lot of extra work for you, but I can feed the horses, at least, and take care of moving them to and from pasture. If it hadn't been for the Scout meeting last night—"

What Chase said under his breath should have earned him a healthy forfeit to the penalty box. "I can handle a little extra work. But I'm thinking that maybe you should try to find a full-time hand, not a part-time one."

Her world took another shift, this time a sickening slide instead of a jolt. "Have you changed your mind about working for me, then?'' *Or just about going to bed with me?*

"Maybe." He made one last lane change, taking one of the spiraling ramps of the clover leaf to get them headed north to Bita Creek. "Maybe I'm feeling a bit trapped, pinned down. I can't very well leave while you don't have anyone else hired, can I?"

She sat there and hated herself for her blasted honesty last night, the honesty that had led her to tell him too much. But she ought to be glad, shouldn't she? She was learning just how quickly he could turn and run the other way when faced with a hint of commitment, and learning it before she'd quite finished falling for him. She could start getting over him right away now.

Soon, at least.

Several silent, crowded miles sped past their closed windows as they left San Antonio. "You sound just like Jimmie," she said at last, as much because she knew he'd hate being compared to another man as because it was true.

"Yeah, well, could be I'm not as different from Jimmie Callaway as I'd like to think." His gaze skimmed her quickly before returning to the highway. "Some men aren't meant for marriage."

He intended for her to take that as a warning, she supposed. "Jimmie played at being a man, but he never quite got there. He never took responsibility for anything, whether it was falling off the bull right out of the chute or making sure his own child had medical attention…much less his niece."

"I knew we'd get to that," he muttered. "Ever since Gonzales shot his mouth off, I knew you'd be bringing that up. Look, it was just money, all right? It wasn't me who sat up with Jennifer when she hurt so bad after a therapy session that she couldn't sleep, because I wasn't there much. I wasn't there.''

"But you cared.''

"So? Money is a damned easy way to care, isn't it? At the time I had plenty of it, and my brother didn't. For years he'd sunk every penny he had into the ranch, fighting just to hold on to it at first, then trying to get it back to where it used to be when our folks were alive. What he didn't have tied up in the ranch, that witch wife of his spent before she took off.''

It was too much information, too fast. Instead of giving Summer the feeling she was getting to know Chase, it reminded her of how little she did know him—in spite of the fact that she'd very nearly let him make love to her last night on her back porch. "Your parents are dead?'' she asked, focusing on the fact that he was about as low on family as she was.

"They were killed in an auto accident when I was eight.'' His forbidding expression bore little resemblance to the laid-back cowboy who'd shown up on her doorstep with Rosie eleven days ago. She knew he considered this subject closed.

Wrong again. "They went out celebrating that night,'' he said unemotionally. "They'd been separated for six months and had just ironed out their differences. Mom was going to move home the next day.''

Oh, God. She bit her lip, hard, to keep from crying.

"The state wouldn't let my brother have custody of me,'' he went on. "He was only sixteen. We had an aunt who was willing to take us in, so we both lived with her a while, but her health was bad. She couldn't handle a hell-raising sixteen-year-old and a screwed-up kid. When she went into the hospital the second time, I went into foster care.'' He took a deep breath, let it

out slowly. "I stayed with nearly a dozen families before I turned seventeen, when my brother finally got
me. For a little while."

Summer thought she had her voice under pretty good
control, but her blasted eyes were still misbehaving. She
blinked rapidly. "You're not telling me this because
you want sympathy. And I don't think you care all that
much if I understand you or not."

From the look he gave her, you'd have thought she
was the one needing sympathy. "You're pretty quick,
aren't you?" he said. "You're right. I told you because
I *don't* need sympathy. See, I didn't really mind after
a while. Once I got over missing my folks, I found out
I liked moving on just fine. Sometimes the changes
were for the better, sometimes not, but when the time
came to go to another family, maybe another town, I
was always ready. And that's the one thing that isn't
going to change, sugar. I'm always going to be ready
to leave."

She swallowed. If he'd been angry or cold or simply
refused to tell her anything about himself, she could
have assumed he was protecting himself, that he did
feel something for her and was fighting it.

But he wasn't fighting anything, was he? He was
being…kind.

Summer thought she might choke on his kindness.
"Are you planning on leaving as soon as I get another
hand? Even though you won't have enough money to
get your truck fixed yet?"

"I haven't decided."

She should have told him right then that it wasn't his
decision. She should have said she wanted him to leave
the minute she could replace him. But she sat there

beside him the rest of the way to the turnoff, feeling sick to her stomach and saying nothing.

"The creek is up," Maud said. She sat at the kitchen table peeling potatoes. The peelings went into a brown grocery sack, the potatoes into a bowl of cold water.

As soon as Summer got home she'd called Maud, who'd kept Ricky that afternoon while Summer and Chase went into San Antonio. Summer had told her to send Ricky home, then invited her to join them for supper. Another meal with just Ricky, Chase and her around the kitchen table would have been too domestic to endure.

Maud, incapable of being a proper guest, had come over early to help fix the meal.

"I imagine it is," Summer said, taking down her cutting board.

"Bill Mosely was saying he hasn't seen it this high since '82, when his pasture flooded."

"We've had a lot of rain this winter." Summer had found that if she kept her upper arm close to her body she could take off her sling long enough to do things like cut up carrots. It wasn't exactly comfortable, but she figured that as long as it didn't hurt, it wasn't doing her any harm. "I haven't been down to see the creek since I fell off that blasted horse."

"I'm sure Chase knows better than to take Ricky too close to the creek," Maud said with an arch look at Summer. "There's one stretch of bank that's pretty badly undercut."

Forty minutes ago Chase had stopped by the back door in his work clothes, including the battered hat that was a distant cousin to the gorgeous Stetson he'd worn to go to San Antonio. He'd told her he was taking Maverick on a short trail ride to test his manners outside the yard. Ricky, who had just finished his math, had talked her and Chase into letting him go along on Honey-Do.

Not that he'd needed to work hard at convincing Chase, who apparently meant it when he said he liked Ricky.

Summer shot her friend an irritated look. "Of course he does."

"It's good that you can trust him."

"You are not exactly subtle, you know that?"

"Subtlety is a waste of time," Maud said, using the end of the peeler to gouge an eye out of the potato, "when you get to be my age. So I'll just come right out and ask if you've watched those two together. Ricky's crazy about Chase, and Chase is as patient with that boy as he is with the ornery gelding that threw you."

"Maud, you have to stop matchmaking."

"I never matchmake." The old woman lied as positively as always, beaming at Summer while she denuded another potato.

"Chase is going to leave. I don't need to hear how good he is with Ricky when he's going to leave."

"A month and a half gives you time to—"

"No, Maud. Now." Summer grabbed a handful of sliced carrots and dropped them into the meat and broth simmering on the stove. "You talked about risks yesterday. Well, I took one. Last night I—well, we'll say I let him know I was interested. Today he let me know he wants me to hurry up and hire another hand. He wants to be free to pick up and go when the urge hits."

Her words came out quick and sharp. They left a

pocket of silence behind, an echoing kind of silence, like after a plate is dropped or a car crashes.

"Sweetie," Maud said, "I'm sorry."

"Don't be," Summer said briskly, heading for the pantry.

"I shouldn't have pushed you to get involved." She shook her head sadly. "A woman gets to be my age, she thinks she can tell a good man when she sees one, but I guess that's vanity."

"Chase *is* a good man." She took out the cornmeal. "That's why, in spite of what he says, he's not going to go, no matter how bad he wants to." She didn't try to keep the bitterness out of her voice. "Not quite yet, anyway."

"I don't understand."

"It's this mess with Ray Fletcher." Summer had already filled Maud in on the details. "I don't think Chase will feel free to leave until he knows for sure about Fletcher. He—I didn't tell you about Chase's niece, did I?"

"No, sweetie, you didn't."

Summer talked as she measured the ingredients for corn bread. "Apparently she's needed a lot of surgery and therapy. He didn't tell me why. He wouldn't have told me that he'd paid for her medical care, either, but Henry Gonzales didn't know it was supposed to be some kind of secret." She rapped an egg on the edge of the bowl. "Chase said it was just money. He seemed to think it didn't count, as if bankrupting himself to pay his niece's medical bills proves what a lousy person he was. I thought he was as stupidly irresponsible as Jimmie, Maud." *Crack* went another egg. "I thought all his winnings had gone to gambling or women or something."

"I guess it came as a shock to learn different, then."
Maud stood and carried the potatoes over to the cutting board.

"He's a good man, just like you thought." She picked up a fork and stirred. "Even if he can't stay, he's a good man."

"If he's so good, he'll stay."

"How old are you claiming to be these days? Seventy-five or so? That's old enough to know life isn't always that simple." The phone rang, interrupting her—which, Summer thought, was just as well. She was too close to snapping at her friend, and for what? For implying Chase wasn't a good man—or for encouraging the stubborn spark of hope inside her, the spark that she and Chase together hadn't been able to smother?

Summer patted her hands dry and reached for the phone as it rang again. That damned spark sat like a sullen coal in her middle, burning. "Hello?"

"Miz Callaway? You don't know me," said a male voice thick with the molasses drawl of the Deep South, "but I heard you're looking for a worker, and I can tell you, ma'am, I do know how to work hard. Bill Mosely down at the feed store told me about the job. I was wonderin' if I could talk to you about it."

Summer's heart jammed in her throat. Soon, very soon, she might find out if she was right about how long Chase would stay.

"Looks too fast for catfish," Chase observed. The big gelding shifted restlessly beneath him. He shortened the reins. They were a good ten feet back of the swollen creek, which was as close as Chase wanted Ricky to get, especially when Chase sat on an undependable horse.

"The fishing's not very good," Ricky admitted. His mount, Honey-Do, was as quiet and mannerly as Maverick was antsy. "It isn't this fast most of the time, though. By July there's hardly any water left, and what there is just crawls along. It's really hot then, too. My birthday's in July."

"Is it?" It occurred to Chase that he wouldn't see this boy turn eight. The thought shouldn't have been startling. It damned sure shouldn't have made Chase's legs tighten around the horse's barrel, cueing the animal to jolt forward. He relaxed his thighs and pulled up on the reins, turning Maverick's head to keep him from dancing any closer to the creek, and apologized with the stroke of one hand for having confused him.

Problem was, Chase was so confused himself he couldn't see straight. "What day?" he asked.

"The fourth." Ricky grimaced. "It's a pain, really, 'cause I have to share my birthday with the whole country."

"Still," Chase said, pressing gently with his knees so that the gelding started walking, "it's not so bad to have the entire country celebrating right along with you, is it?"

"I guess not." Ricky gave Honey-Do a nudge, and the mare stepped out smartly alongside Maverick. "Do you like to fish?"

"Now and again."

"Me, too. Mom does, too, but...you remember how I said my dad died when I was little?"

Uh-oh. "I remember."

"Well, it was a long time ago, an' I was just two, so it doesn't bother me, except sometimes...you know, it would just be kind of neat to have a dad around to do stuff. Like fishing, you know, or just...stuff."

"You've mentioned your Uncle Billy, your dad's brother. He does things with you sometimes, doesn't he?"

"Yeah, but he's gone a lot, with the rodeo. And…it's not the same."

God help them both, it sounded like Rick was wanting *him* for a father. Dammit, he did not need this. First the woman and now her son—winding their emotions around him, wrapping him in feelings that threatened to tie him up tight as a bulldogged steer.

Ten feet away, the creek splashed its hasty way downstream, making enough racket to drown out the sound of the horses' hooves clomping along on the damp ground. Chase's emotions were crowding him about as much as that noisy stream was crowding its banks. "My dad died, too," he said at last. "I was older than you when it happened. I had to live with other families then, and you're right. Some of the dads in those families were nice guys, but it never was the same."

Neither of them spoke for a while. Chase turned the gelding's head toward home, and they'd started back across the biggest field between them and the house when Rick asked, in a small voice, "So do you think one dad is all a guy ever gets? Like, I mean, if someone doesn't start out as your dad, he can't ever be your dad?"

"No. No, that's not what I mean. Sometimes people get another chance at having a dad. It doesn't happen all the time, though." He looked at the boy riding beside him. Ricky sat a horse well, keeping his heels down and his slight body balanced over the withers.

Chase wasn't surprised by Ricky's skill. Summer was good at a lot of things, like training horses, teaching little kids to ride and putting together the kind of meals that gave "home cooking" its glowing reputation. What she was best at, though, absolutely aces at, was being a mother. "You can't count on it happening, Rick, but that doesn't mean you should give up. Do you get what I mean?" *Don't give up—just don't count on me to fill those dreams.*

Ricky's face brightened. "I think so. Like when you try out for the team. Not everyone gets to be on it, but that doesn't mean you shouldn't try."

"Pretty much, except that you can't get a dad by trying, the way you might get on the team by practicing. Life doesn't always bend the way we want it to. Sometimes," he said, "life doesn't bend at all, and that's when people get hurt. If life won't bend and we won't turn loose, something's going to break. It's like riding a horse who's doing his darnedest to throw you—you have to stay loose, and you have to know how to get off when the time comes."

Ricky didn't say a word, and Chase was certain he'd blown it. Ricky was so silent. The kid was *never* silent. Chase must have really screwed up.

By the time he bent to unfasten the gate opening into the smaller field, he'd decided he would definitely move on as soon as Summer got another hand hired. He'd keep in touch with Henry Gonzales, do what he could to get Summer out of this situation she was in, but he'd do it from a little ways away.

His leaving would hurt Ricky. The idea gave him a peculiar sort of pain, the sort that he supposed was reserved for those who hurt the truly innocent. But it would be worse for the boy if he stayed. He was sure of that.

"You know, Chase, I'm not sure about that bending

stuff," Ricky said seriously, as Honey-Do followed Maverick through the gate. "I mean, staying loose makes sense. You have to stay loose in the saddle to move with the horse. But staying loose isn't the same as turning loose, is it?"

Chase opened his mouth, then closed it when he realized he didn't have an answer. All the rest of the way to the house, he didn't have an answer.

When they got to the house, he forgot the question. Summer stood on the back porch talking to a short, red-haired man with a grin like a grown-up Opie from Mayberry. Chase got a good look at the man as he and Ricky rode close to the porch on their way to the stable, and he got a good look at Summer's face. Her expression looked calm enough, but he was certain he saw feelings underneath. Anxiety? Or excitement?

He didn't want her feeling either one, dammit, not for that oversize boy on the porch with her.

He didn't realize he'd unconsciously pulled Maverick to a stop until Ricky reined in beside him. "Do you reckon that's the new hand Mom was going to hire?" he asked.

"Yeah," he said softly. It's what he'd told her to do, wasn't it? What she needed to do. So he could move on. "Yeah, I guess that's probably who he is," Chase said, wanting to hit someone. "Her new hand."

Eight

"Wayne seems like he'll make a decent hand," Summer said, stretching to put the big china bowl back on the top shelf.

Chase stood at the sink, scrubbing the pan the stew had been in. "He doesn't know a damned thing about horses."

He sounded angry. Summer herself felt half-sick with dread, working alongside Chase in her small kitchen for what might be the last time...and stingingly aware of him. Ricky was in the living room, watching TV, but Chase had made a point of staying in the kitchen to help her clean up after supper.

She knew why. He had something to tell her.

She wished he'd go ahead and say it. He was leaving, wasn't he? She'd been wrong about him staying until Ray Fletcher's involvement in her troubles was either stopped or disproven. He was going to leave right away, and that's why he was on edge. Hadn't she seen it over and over with Jimmie? When the urge to move on got too strong, he'd pick a fight. That way he wouldn't feel so guilty for leaving.

Damned if she'd fight with Chase and give him the excuse he wanted. She inhaled deeply and opened the subject they'd both been avoiding. "Wayne's coming in tomorrow at four. If you're staying, I'll have him take over some of the kennel work, and you can handle the stable. If not, he can clean the stable and the kennel, and I'll do the feeding. It'll work out. He's willing to take either part-time or full-time work."

"And just why is that?" The pan Chase had just washed and rinsed thudded down on the counter a little too hard. "He can't possibly live on what he'd make working part-time."

"I doubt he can live on what he'd get for full-time," she said dryly. Summer glanced around the kitchen. Everything was done except for drying the pans Chase had washed. Reluctantly she joined him by the sink, opened the cabinet and took out a dish towel. "Wayne was honest with me about his plans. He's going to be looking for a better job while he works for me, and I can't fault him for that. He promised to give me notice when he gets something else lined up, and he'd like to stay on part-time if he can. Maybe by then my collarbone will be healed, and I won't need anyone full-time anymore."

All the pans were clean. Chase grabbed the cutting board and started scrubbing it. His sleeves were rolled up past the elbows, and his muscular forearms were dark with the year-round tan of a working man and dusted with bleached blond hair. She wanted to touch his arm. Just one touch, she thought—just so she'd

know how that tanned skin felt or the hollow of his
elbow. Or his hand. If she could touch his hand....
They'd kissed, but she'd never held his hand.

He scowled. "I suppose you believed him."

Summer shrugged her good shoulder. Actually, she
couldn't make herself care whether Wayne Redringer
worked for her for a week or a year. Or if he worked
for her at all, except that his presence would make it
possible for Chase to leave.

She did care about that. Too much. She moved over
to the stove to put the corn bread pan away.

"Did he have references?" Chase asked. "A woman
who lives alone like you do can't hire just anyone."
He was still scouring that cutting board as if he intended
to sand it down to a spatula.

"Of course he has references. I called them before
he came out to interview. I left a message at one number, and spoke to one of his former employers, a res-
taurant owner in Georgia. The man recommended him
highly—though he said Wayne has a touch of wander-
lust and probably won't stay." *No more than you will.*
She came back to the sink and began to dry the last
pan one-handed.

At last Chase rinsed the cutting board and turned off
the water. Silence rolled in between them with the loss
of that small sound, but it was the heat, the edgy, mer-
ciless heat she felt from standing so near him, that
forced her to speak. "Am I going to be here alone, then,
Chase? Are you leaving?"

"You know I am."

But was he leaving *now?* And why didn't he tell her?
He knew, he must know, what she was asking.

"Mom?" Ricky said from the doorway. "Is something wrong?"

She took a deep breath, grappling for a steadiness she didn't feel. "Nope, not a thing."

"Oh." Ricky looked from one of them to the other. "Well, the phone rang and you'd left it in the living room, so I guess you didn't hear." He crossed the kitchen and held the cordless phone out to Chase. "It's for you. I think it's your brother."

Chase looked surprised as he took it.

His brother, Summer thought. The man whose little girl could walk now because her uncle had earned plenty of money in the rodeo, until he got too busted up to keep competing. The brother Chase loved but hadn't been allowed to stay with when their parents died. Instead he'd been shuffled from place to place, person to person, until there was no part of him that believed in stability anymore.

All of a sudden the pieces settled into place for Summer—quick, smooth, inevitable. Chase didn't keep moving on down the road because he wanted to. He did it because he had to—because he didn't know how to stop.

Chase said something cheerfully insulting to his brother. Summer heard the love behind the banter. Her chest ached, and she remembered to breathe. It felt as if her heart expanded with her breath. As if she were breathing with her heart instead of her lungs.

God, she hurt. "Come on, Rick," she said. "We'll let Chase have some privacy."

"I was just going to get a snack." He made for the refrigerator, obviously wanting to hang around and eavesdrop.

"Later. Come on, now." Corraling her nosy son with one hand on his shoulder, she steered him back into the living room, where the TV greeted her with canned laughter.

She knew what she had to do now. She just had to find the nerve—and the right nightgown.

At 11:05 that night the skies were clear of clouds. The moon was nearly full, and the stars blazed gloriously overhead while Summer stood at the door to the kennel and tried not to hyperventilate.

She was cold. Her white cotton nightgown was the only one she owned with a matching robe, the only one that might be considered remotely romantic. It was plain, but it was also ankle length and thin enough to be sheer without the robe—and cold even with the robe.

At least the robe hid the upper portion of her stupid clavicle brace, which the gown didn't. She'd decided reluctantly that she'd better leave it on since she wasn't using the sling. She kept her left arm protectively close to her body. Cradled unromantically in that arm was a walkie-talkie. She'd left the other one in Ricky's room by his bed—a system she'd worked out long ago for the nights when she had to be up with a sick horse, but didn't want to leave Ricky completely alone. She'd left Kelpie in the house, too. The dog was no doubt curled up at Ricky's feet by now.

She shivered. It would, she told herself, at least be warmer inside the kennel's office. Her hand shook when she lifted the keys to the door, but she managed to get the right key in the doorknob and turn it.

As soon as the door swung open, one of the dogs in the runs in the main section of the kennel let out a low, sleepy woof. She froze. If the dogs woke up and started barking—if Chase heard them and came out here to see what was up—she shuddered. She would look so ridiculous.

What was wrong with her? This was insane.

So she was nuts, she thought, taking a deep breath. Okay. She was still going to do this. If Chase saw her creeping toward his room in the dark—well, she hadn't really thought she could come over here and climb into his bed without him noticing, had she? Though it seemed better, somehow, if she could reach his room while he was still asleep. If she were touching him when he woke up and saw her, she wouldn't be quite so scared.

Chase wouldn't laugh at her. She knew that. Even if he sent her away, he wouldn't laugh. Summer took a step, then another, into the darkened room, finding her way past the desk more by memory than sight.

He might be kind, though. Oh, God, what if he was *kind* again?

When she walked into the metal trash can by the desk, it made enough racket to wake Sleeping Beauty without the prince's help. The Brauns' poodle yipped excitedly, joined immediately by the Kepperlings' Schnauzer and then by at least half the dogs being boarded.

Summer turned and fled.

At least, she tried to flee, but someone moved a wall into her path. She smacked right up against it—a hard, hot…naked…wall. She was pretty sure about the naked part, since her hand rested on a bare chest. Then one big, warm hand grasped her right shoulder while another, careful of her injured side, slipped to her waist and held on.

"No way are you leaving," Chase's voice said, low and dangerous, near her ear. "You shouldn't have

come, Summer, and I guess you figured that out, but
you got smart too late. I told you how I am about temptation. There's no way I'm letting you leave, now that
you're here.''

Leave? Oh, no. Not with Chase so warm, so close,
so…bare. Her hand rose, threaded through his hair, and
she urged his head down. Their lips met and closed the
connection.

He was gentle with her mouth for about two hurried-
up heartbeats. Then he got serious.

Lightning couldn't have felt any hotter or done any
more damage than his tongue when it came prowling
inside her mouth. He tasted like the storms they'd been
plagued with lately, like wind and thunder—thunder
that she must have swallowed, because she felt it rumbling up from her belly, shaking her world. ''Chase,''
she gasped when his mouth left hers to race over her
face as if he were starved for her taste. She looped her
arm firmly around his neck so she wouldn't fall down.
''Chase, I sure do hope you have birth control, because
I don't, and you—you are going to take me to bed,
aren't you?''

He actually chuckled, right there in the middle of that
storm. ''Oh, yes,'' he said softly. ''Yes to both.''

He bent and swung her up into his arms. She clutched
the walkie-talkie to her chest and dropped her keys.
Maybe his night vision was better than hers, or maybe
he was luckier. He didn't run into anything.

Once across his threshold, there was light. He'd
tucked the curtains up on the rod so that all of the night
streamed into the room—starshine and cool white
moonlight. He stopped next to his narrow bed and set
her carefully on the floor, and for a moment they stood
there quietly, leaning up against each other. His arms

were loose around her waist. Her left arm lay between them—oh, but she was getting tired of that—while her right hand curved possessively around his arm.

She didn't know why he hesitated. She couldn't imagine that he was dizzy the way she was, more moon silly than she'd ever been at sixteen and twice as scared as when she gave up her virginity. Her heart pounded, and her body ached.

"Summer," he said at last, and touched his forehead to hers. "I'm not going to stop. Not unless you can be pretty damn convincing about wanting me to, and then I'll do my best to change your mind. But I need to know what you're doing here."

That was one question she knew the answer to. "Seducing you," she said, and turned to set the walkie-talkie on the chest of drawers. "You were supposed to seduce me, but you were taking too long about it."

His arms tightened, drawing her securely up against him. "I don't think seduction is going to be necessary," he said dryly.

"Oh...my." He *was* naked. All-over naked.

He held her close, and his voice was hoarse when he asked, "Aren't you going to ask me if I'm leaving in the morning?"

"No." She tipped her head back so she could see him better. He looked so serious in the moonlight, with all the dips and crags of his face dusted with silver and shadows. "I won't say it doesn't matter. It does. But once I understood what I was risking by staying away, I had to come to you." Because he might really leave tomorrow. She'd understood that suddenly, listening to him talk to the brother he obviously loved yet had left a thousand miles behind. Chase might leave her without her ever knowing what it was like to lie with him.

It was a risk she hadn't been able to take.

His mouth smiled. She thought his eyes might have been smiling, too, but they were in shadow, unreadable in the moonglow. "I'm not going to ask if you know what you're doing," he said, threading his fingers through her hair. "Obviously you lost your mind. I ought to be sorry, but I only hope you don't get it back too soon."

When he bent, he stroked the side of her head with his in a curiously tender gesture. Then his lips touched the joining of her neck and shoulder, and lightning struck. She jumped.

"Shh," he said, petting her hip through the thin layers of cotton. "Gently, sweetheart. I couldn't stand it if I hurt you."

"I don't feel...calm."

"Now, me, I'm feeling as calm as any stallion does in the spring, when the mares come into heat," he said, his mouth moving deliciously around to the hollow of her throat, "but we have to be careful with you." He straightened, and his hands went to her hair again. Carefully he arranged it the way he wanted it, smoothing it behind her shoulders.

Then his right hand went to the front of her robe and unfastened the first button. With the next button, his knuckles skimmed her breast. Her breath caught. She let go of his shoulder so she could support her left arm, holding it out so he could get to the buttons. "I wish— I wish I wasn't hurt."

"I wish you weren't hurt, too, sweetheart." His knuckles brushed her breast again, and lingered, making small circles. "But I'm going to enjoy taking real good care of you." His grin flashed white. As he spoke he moved his hand and rubbed her nipple with those hard, scarred knuckles.

Sensation spun from her nipple throughout her body. She gasped. Her attention spiraled in—to that one place, where his knuckle rubbed up and down through the thin cotton.

"It's going to be good, Summer," he promised, his voice low and husky. "I'm going to make it so very good for you."

Chase was painfully aware of how little he promised with those words as he continued to tease her sweet, hard little nipple. He hadn't even promised to be there for her tomorrow—but she hadn't asked for it, had she? She'd come to him without asking for anything except this, the heat and madness.

He still couldn't believe it. He'd been standing at his window, staring out, so torn and twisted inside he hadn't even tried to sleep after he'd stripped for bed, when he'd heard the sound of a key in the lock of the office door. Thinking it might be one of Fletcher's people, he'd moved into the office silently, and positioned himself in the darkest shadows. Ready.

Then the door had swung open. He'd seen her standing there, silhouetted against the moonlit night with the shape of her body just visible beneath the long, virginal white gown.

She'd come to him.

He'd gone hard so fast he hadn't dared speak or move, afraid he'd lose control.

It took all his concentration now to move from one button to the next instead of ripping the robe and gown from her. "You cold, sweetheart?" he asked when a shiver took her.

"No," she said, and her voice was sweet to him, low

and husky. "Not anymore. Chase? The most comfortable position for my collarbone…is lying down. I can
touch you then, too, instead of having to hold my arm."

He froze. Then he took her head in both hands and
kissed her, taking her mouth the way he wanted to take
her body, hard and deep and wild. When he straightened his head he was back in control. Mostly. He even
smiled. Barely. "Let's get you naked."

She was self-conscious about her brace, but not her
nudity. She stood before him in the moonlight, pale and
naked and strong. Her hair was long and wild and, in
this dreamy light, several shades darker than the cream
of her skin. Her hips were skinny, her breasts were
beautiful, and he longed to taste the dark berries at their
crests. He made himself wait until she was lying down,
stretched out on the hard mattress of his narrow bed.

Summer lay in Chase's bed and looked at him standing there, his body lean and strong and perfect, and
reached for him with her good arm. He came down over
her, propping himself up on one elbow to keep his
weight away from the upper half of her body. He kissed
and suckled and touched. She touched, too, and licked
whatever part of him came close enough, and tried to
remember to breathe with her mouth as well as her
heart.

And in that bare room, in that hot, crowded bed, with
the two of them bathed in the chilly glow of the moon,
Chase did what he'd said he couldn't bear to do. He
hurt her, over and over—a thousand tiny, startling pains
like the pins-and-needles sensation of walking on a foot
that's been asleep—pains that came because of his care,
not in spite of it—because he trembled, his muscles
rigid with control. Because his breath came hard with
need. Because his expression was fierce, but his hands

were gentle, and he wouldn't rush, wouldn't take the least chance with her injury.

At last she could do nothing but say his name over and over, wanting him inside her until she was blind to everything else. And even then he was slow and cautious, this man who'd spent years risking himself. He paused to sheath himself, and entered her slowly.

It was just as well he did, too. She was tight, absurdly so for a woman who'd born a child, but it had been a long time. So long.

"There, sweetheart, there," he crooned to her or maybe to himself, to keep his entry as smooth and easy as possible as he slid in, a little at a time. "There," he said again as he at last buried himself fully, firmly within. She shuddered with a richness of feeling, as if life itself had poured down from the stars to flood her, body and soul. It didn't matter that she could hold him with only one arm, when she held and loved him with her whole body.

She felt him shudder, too. And then he began to move. There was no more room for thought, only feelings...sensations...sounds. His groans and hers. The fleshy noises of their joining, the quick murmurs of praise and glory—the sensation of hanging on desperately at the very edge of a precipice at the same time that she raced towards that edge as hard and fast as she could go.

"That's it, sweetheart," he urged, as breathless as she, his left hand clasping her right. "That's it, let go, just let go. I'm here."

She did. And he was there, falling right behind her, calling her name as they tumbled off the edge of the world together.

Later, when the world had whirled back down into

place, Chase lay on his side, curled around her, one of his legs thrown over both of hers. He didn't speak, but one of his hands toyed with her hair. Summer lay very still on her back, the only position her injury permitted.

She loved him. Silly of her to have thought she had time to talk herself out of it, as if love were any easier to reason with than any other of life's essentials, like rain or fire or the slow turning of one season into another. Summer lay there brimful of love and the first pangs of grief over the loss to come, still quivering with aftershocks from the pleasure he'd given her. She was sure something would spill out if she moved.

Something like the words that she knew, once spoken, would send him away from her.

Peace and certainty evaporated quietly, like the dew once the sun's up. She lay there a few more minutes, wishing she could put her head on his chest and listen to his heart. When she felt tears press at the backs of her eyes, stupid, sorry-for-herself tears because she might live her whole life without hearing Chase's heartbeat in just that way, she knew it was time to go.

"I'll walk you back," he said when she sat up. Neither of them spoke much, but he took her hand. They held hands as they walked across the grassy yard under a sky splendid with stars, and that, she thought, was a moment worth whatever happened tomorrow.

She almost believed it.

At her back porch they drifted to a stop together, near the door. She turned to face him, glad of the darkness there in the shadows under the roof. Her heart was so full of questions she didn't doubt they'd be leaking out of her eyes, plain for him to see. If it weren't so dark.

He cupped her face in his two hands and tilted it up. Instead of kissing her mouth, though, he pressed his lips to her forehead. His breath was warm on her skin. "I'm not leaving tomorrow," he said softly. "But I will go. Don't fool yourself into hoping for anything different from me."

And Summer, safe in that concealing darkness, looked right at him and lied as positively as ever Maud had. "I'm not," she said, and turned and went inside.

Nine

Chase drifted awake about six the next morning. He was hard and throbbing. His hand moved across the sheet beside him, reaching for Summer.

When he realized what he'd done, he bolted out of bed. He went straight to the cramped shower stall, where he washed away the traces of their lovemaking, removing her scent from his body.

Washing off her scent wasn't going to be enough. He knew that. But it was all he could do right now. He couldn't leave yet, not until he knew Summer and her land were safe from Fletcher's manipulations. Fletcher was smart, he was ruthless, and he wanted to be in Henry Gonzales's league—but he wasn't. Not by a long shot. The way Chase saw it, a man like that might back off, once he knew Gonzales was onto him. So it might be no more than a few days before Chase could move on, having appeased whatever scraps of conscience he had left by that time.

The shower did wash away her scent, but it didn't have much effect on his groin. He wanted to be *in* her. He wanted Summer, dammit. Not just a climax. The difference was distinct, and unwelcome.

As he pulled on his clothes, grimacing at the difficulty of dressing while a certain body part remained stubbornly hard, he wondered how long he'd have to wait. He'd told her he wasn't leaving yet, but he hadn't told her he meant to have her as often as possible in however many days they had together. In spite of what he'd seen last night.

Chase had unusually good night vision. He'd seen what was in her eyes when they'd stood on her back porch, and he knew what name to put to it. But he wasn't going to, not even to himself. Especially not to himself.

Summer was able to fasten her bra that morning for the first time since her accident. She put it on after taking a quick, early shower. With the bra around her waist like a belt, she hooked it together in front, then slid it around. Getting her arms through the straps and pulling it up wasn't exactly comfortable, but it didn't hurt.

The bra was a small mark of returning independence. She tried to take some pleasure in it, but felt only a perverse stubbornness.

He isn't leaving today.

That meant she still had time. Time for what, she didn't know—she was no good at changing a man. She knew better than to try. But she had this feeling about Chase....

Well, she thought, amused with herself as she wiped
the shower's steam from the bathroom mirror, she had
that feeling, all right. She was tender and a little sore
this morning…and tingly. Definitely tingly.

But she had another feeling, too. It might have been
based more on pure hope than reality, but she had the
idea that maybe Chase wasn't really born to wander—
that maybe somewhere deep inside he wanted roots, but
didn't quite know how to settle in.

Summer brushed her teeth, put on a little mascara
and blush and brushed her hair. Then she pulled on a
cotton shirtwaist dress and that blasted blue sling and
headed out of the bathroom.

It was Sunday and she intended to go to church later,
but right now she needed to see the man who'd become
her lover last night.

Not that he'd said anything about continuing their
intimacy. She'd warned him, though, hadn't she? She
had plans of her own. And at least, she told herself as
she left the bathroom, she didn't have to compete with
the rodeo this time.

Ricky was still asleep when the back door closed
behind her.

The whickers of the horses told her he was in the
stable, and that's where she found him, distributing the
last bale of alfalfa hay among the older horses. He had
on jeans faded nearly white and a shirt in the same
shape, his old boots and no hat. Early morning sunshine
slanted in through the stalls on the east side of the stable, lighting up the dancing dust motes and landing, soft
as springtime, on Chase's craggy face and six-shades-
of-blond hair.

Her heart gave a little kick, and she wanted, absurdly,
just to stand there and look at him. Nothing else.

He looked up. She started toward him, but his stillness and silence made the smile she offered him uncertain.

She stopped in front of him.

"You look a little too dressed up for helping me with the horses," he said at last, one corner of his mouth turning up. "A bit too dressy for me to kiss good morning, too, considering how dirty I am."

He did still want to kiss her, then. Tension eased from her shoulders and spine, letting the morning sunshine spread through her warmly. "So kiss me carefully."

Now he smiled fully. "Yes, ma'am."

He didn't touch her except with his lips, tongue, and teeth. He was slow and thorough, and when he lifted his head, her eyes were closed and her breath unsteady.

"Take off that pretty dress," he suggested, low and husky, "so I don't get it dirty."

Slowly her eyelids lifted. His mouth was wet from hers, his eyes hooded. She liked that. She wanted him to ache the way she did.

But that aching wasn't going to do either of them any good this morning. She sighed and stepped back, so that he wasn't quite so easy to reach for. "It's important for me to be at church today. If I don't show up, people will think I'm ashamed because of that article. I need to make it to Sunday school, too—that's when I'll be able to talk to the most people—and I'm nowhere near ready."

He began separating one strand of her hair from the rest. "You going to tell everyone how unlikely it would be for Fletcher to be behind your problems?"

"Like Henry Gonzales said?" Her eyebrows drew

together. "I like the idea, but we don't know that he's responsible."

"And that's what you'll be telling people. That you're just sure it isn't him." He lifted the strand of hair to his face. "Your hair smells like strawberries again."

There was something irresistibly erotic about watching him smell her hair. She couldn't move, caught by more than the light tether of her hair. "Could you—would you mind keeping an eye on Ricky while I'm gone?"

"He's not going with you?" Lazily Chase rubbed her hair under his chin, up his jaw, watching her closely with his smiling eyes.

She felt the tickles along her own skin. "Today is an official 'lazy day.' That's one of our deals, see. As long as he keeps his grades up he gets to pick one Sunday a month to be lazy."

"Yeah?" Now he brushed the vee of skin revealed at the top of his shirt with her hair.

Her eyes followed his hand. "On a lazy day he doesn't have to get dressed until noon or make up his bed, go to Sunday school, or do any but the real basic stuff, like brushing his teeth and feeding his pets. He's…still asleep."

"How about that," he said softly. He reached out, and now it was the skin of her throat he stroked with the brush made from her own hair. Chills chased along her skin. "I'll be glad to keep an eye on Rick. Do you think he'll sleep much longer?" He dipped the soft brush inside the bodice of her dress and teased the flesh along the tops of her right breast.

Her breath caught. She wished suddenly, fervently, she hadn't put the sling on. It was in the way. "He should.'' Ricky would sleep for another hour, probably two…and she didn't really have to go to Sunday school as well as church, did she? "He was up late last night."

"So were we, weren't we…ma'am?" His eyes were pure wickedness, laughing at her. "Now, was there anything else you'd like me to do? Any other little chores," he asked, tickling her breast again with her own hair, "that you'd like me to take care of for you?"

Oh, Lord, she wanted to wiggle. "Maybe." Feeling daring, Summer gave him a sultry look. "Maybe I do have one other little chore for you. It's—awfully warm in here."

His smile widened while his eyes got that sleepy look. "You know, I was just thinking that very thing. You want me to help you cool off a little?"

She nodded.

"Well, then." He dropped the strand of hair he'd been teasing her with, and his fingers went to the buttons on her dress. "I guess the first thing would be to let you get a little more air on your skin. That ought to cool you off."

"The sling—"

He shook his head firmly. "No, you need that sling." He'd gotten the top two buttons undone—without touching her, dammit. She frowned. "Of course, if it stays on, we'll have to find some other places to expose to the air, won't we?"

"That makes sense," she agreed breathlessly as his hands went down the row of buttons, working more quickly now, until her dress gaped open to the waist.

She expected him to stop there. He didn't. Instead, he dropped to his knees and continued to undo buttons…one after another…after another…all the way down. He didn't look at her face. He looked where his hands were busy.

"There, now," he said when her dress hung open all the way down. "Is that better, ma'am?" He smiled—but it wasn't her face he was smiling at.

Summer wasn't wearing a slip. There was only a thin bit of nylon where he was looking—red nylon with a bit of lace. Her face heated along with her body. "It's odd," she said, her voice gone husky, "but I'm just not cooling off."

"No?" Now he looked up at her. His eyes, she thought, were the most alive thing she'd ever seen—mirthful, wicked eyes, filled equally with hunger and mischief. "I have to say I'm at a loss." He dropped his hands to his sides. "What do you want me to do next?"

Summer didn't know how to answer. She throbbed—right where he'd been looking, and in other places, too—and she could think of a lot of things she'd like him to do about it. But she couldn't *say* those things. "It's your fault," she told him reproachfully. "The way you're looking at me makes me...hot."

"I'm sure sorry about that, but I don't see how I can stop. I mean, you're standing there with your dress open, letting me see all that soft skin of yours, not to mention your pretty red panties." He sighed. "I'm only human."

Her lips twitched. "You could close your eyes."

"No, ma'am." He shook his head firmly. "No. While I'm trying to be a real good hand and do just what you want, I've got my standards. Believe me, closing my eyes at this point would definitely violate them. But I tell you what." He straightened, bringing his head level with her belly, and his hands went to the backs of her knees—and up, along her thighs, until he held her firmly just beneath her bottom. "We'll see what a little evaporative cooling can do." And he put his mouth on her stomach and licked her.

This time she did squirm. And giggle.

"Ticklish?" He paused and blew on the wet path left by his tongue.

She shivered. Exquisite sensations raced over her— prickles as tender as new grass in the spring. Hunger as sharp and cutting as a north wind in winter. She clutched at his shoulder. "Chase—?"

"Well, now," he said, kissing her belly again, "I must be doing something right this time, if you're shivering. Cooling off now?" He blew on her again.

"Not…exactly."

This time, when he leaned forward to lick and kiss her, his fingers hooked the sides of her panties, and with one smooth gesture he had them down around her ankles. She yelped in surprise but had no time to be embarrassed, because his hands, so careful last night and this morning, were suddenly ruthless.

He pushed her legs apart. Off balance physically and emotionally, she instinctively tried to shove him away. He ignored that. His forearms kept her legs apart, his hair bristly against the sensitive skin of her inner thighs, while his hands parted her intimately. His head dipped.

She tried to shove his head back. No one had ever done such a thing to her, not in a stable, not anywhere, and to stand there, pinned, held immobile by the strength in his arms while he explored her this way, was more than she could handle.

Then his mouth met her. His tongue. Two seconds later her free hand disconnected from her brain. Her whole body, in fact, had to make do suddenly without any guidance, because her brain had fried. That busy hand of hers wasn't trying to push him away anymore, but was grasping his hair, clutching him, urging him on. And her body didn't miss her brain at all, because it was burning itself up as greedily as any fire ever consumed the wood it fed on.

Chase took her swiftly, inexorably, to the edge. Without a shred of compunction, he pushed her over.

And kept kissing her. When her muscles were too limp to keep her standing on her own, his arms held her up, and he kissed her. More gently now—lapping at her, penetrating her—bringing her rapidly from what should have been satiation back to a need as keen as if she hadn't already grabbed the stars once.

Then he stopped.

"Chase?"

"Hang on, sweetheart."

Her eyes focused. She saw him unbuttoning his shirt hastily. He threw it on the dirt floor of the stable and reached for her. He sat on the shirt, pulling her down with him.

She got the idea pretty quickly this time and straddled him, her knees on the soft cotton of his shirt. The position felt incredibly wanton, sitting astride his clothed lower body with her tender parts exposed to the soft, worn denim of his jeans.

Denim that was being mightily strained at the moment. She wiggled.

He groaned. "Take it easy."

The feeling of power that flooded her, pure, erotic power, was as brand-new as the utter vulnerability of a few minutes before had been. And just as delicious. She might have played around in the shallows with this sort of feeling when she was young, she realized, but she'd barely gotten her ankles wet. Marriage had put a stop to her flirting—and not just with others, but with her husband, too. Jimmie hadn't liked her to be "unlady-like."

Jimmie, she understood now, hadn't been able to handle having her splash in the shallows of a woman's sexual power, much less test the deeper waters. But Chase had tossed her in willy-nilly, over her head. And jumped in after her.

She smiled at him, a slow, wicked smile, while her hand made a casual journey down his chest. "Easy," she said, "isn't how I want it at all."

She moved against him again, hearing him groan and loving that, loving the way his hands tightened at her waist. Loving him. Chase had found one of the few positions that would work for her without hurting her collarbone. A surge of love made her hand as tender as her eyes were wicked when she pulled down his zipper. "You seem kind of overheated yourself," she said, smiling as she stroked him and shifted, getting ready to take him inside her. "Let's see what we can do about that." She took him inside her and gasped. He grinned and pressed up, his voice wickedly husky when he said, "Ride 'em, cowgirl!" She did—right past the sunset and off into the stars.

Summer made it to church that morning, but not Sunday school. She mentioned to a couple of people after the service that she didn't believe Ray Fletcher could be behind her recent misfortunes, and they took her assurances exactly the way Henry Gonzales had expected them to.

By the time she left she was pretty sure which of her neighbors had complained to the SPCA and the paper.

Dwight Robbin had a small pecan orchard bordering the southwest end of her property. Thelma from the Cut 'n' Curl said he'd been going around telling people how he was sure that article was the absolute truth. He'd said it so often, Thelma assured Summer, that hardly anyone believed him. And once the SPCA went ahead and investigated and found nothing wrong, why, everyone would know the old grouch was still trying to get back at her over the boundary dispute he'd had with her father all those years ago.

So when Summer turned her Toyota down the highway leading home, she was feeling hopeful. When she reached Three Oaks, her lover and her son surprised her by having lunch ready. Ricky's contribution was peanut butter and jelly sandwiches, while Chase had fixed lemonade and a lopsided chocolate cake. She was so happy she thought something would bust.

On Monday the SPCA brought inspectors in from San Antonio to check out Summer's facilities. Their report completely exonerated her, and the newspaper promised to run an article about it. Tuesday morning she found a good source for more alfalfa hay. A friend of a friend, one of those wealthy men whose ranch is more hobby than investment, had planted and baled extra alfalfa and hadn't bothered to sell the excess hay to a feed store.

They didn't hear from Henry Gonzales on Monday, Tuesday or Wednesday.

On Thursday the sun was shining, the dishwater was hot and slippery with suds, and the man standing behind Summer, his hands on her hips, was just plain hot. And Summer was happy.

"Summer," Chase said, exasperated, "I told you I'd get the pan."

"I don't mind." She scrubbed with her right hand at a place where the lasagna she'd warmed up for their lunch had bonded permanently with the glass.

"You're not supposed to have your arm out of the sling so much."

"As long as it doesn't hurt, I don't figure I'm doing myself any harm." Summer was guiltily aware that her collarbone was starting to ache, however. "I'm almost finished."

Chase gave a put-upon sigh. "You just like being persuaded. Well, a man's work is never done," he said, and bent to kiss the side of her neck.

Desire spread like warm syrup through her veins, thick and sticky. She made an approving sound.

"Let go of the pan, Summer," Chase murmured into her neck.

She smiled. He was right. She did like being persuaded.

Chase didn't play fair. He brought his body up against hers, trapping her between him and the sink, her hands in the hot, sudsy water, his body now pressing against hers, now rubbing in slow, mesmerizing rhythm. "Foul play," she said, and turned into his arms, circling his neck with her good arm, dripping soapy water down his back.

He was smiling when he bent to kiss her.

Their lips met and lingered softly. *There's time for this,* Summer thought. Surely they had time to enjoy the slow and sweet moments as well as the ragged nighttime passion when they took each other, hard and fierce, in the dark. Every night she went to him, and every night she found enough joy to balance the desperation. And in the days...

He raised his head and looked a question at her.

She loosened the fingers that had clenched in his shirt, and made herself smile. "So, did you fix the light switch in the hall?" In the days she was happy. In spite of the worry, in spite of everything, she was happy—except for the time every morning between the moment when she woke up alone in her own bed and the moment when she first saw Chase. Because she didn't know. Until she saw him each day, she never knew if that might be the day he would leave.

Shadows lurked behind the smiles her lover gave her now, and she hated that. He was a good man, and he was sure he was going to hurt her, and the knowledge put ghosts in his eyes.

He smiled at her now. "You didn't know what a bargain you were getting when you hired me, did you?" He shook his head. "You should have replaced that switch a long time ago, Summer. When anything electrical gets hot to the touch when it's turned on, there's something wrong."

She shrugged one shoulder. "I quit using it."

Now he was frowning. "That's not good enough. When you—"

The ringing of the phone interrupted what she suspected was going to be a lecture. "I'd better answer that."

"Your hands are still wet," he said, turning her loose reluctantly, "according to the back of my shirt. I'll get it—if I can find it." He followed the sound of the ringing down the hall toward the living room.

Summer felt a niggle of apprehension. Jimmie's mother had called yesterday to ask if the rumors she'd heard were true. It hadn't been a pleasant conversation. Nor had Eloise Callaway been the only one to call, curious about—or condemning—Summer's rumored involvement with her hired hand.

Somehow it hadn't occurred to Summer that she and Chase would become the subject of gossip. It should have, of course. She turned back to the sink. She boarded a lot of animals here, so a lot of people came and went every day. Somehow she and Chase had given themselves away. Maybe with a glance. Maybe a quick touch. Maybe, she thought, flushing, the expression on her face when she looked at him told everyone all they needed to know.

She paused before reaching for the faucet, waiting to see if the phone was for her. When she heard the low murmur of Chase's voice, she relaxed and turned the water on.

Summer hadn't blamed Eloise for being upset. The woman was worried about Ricky, who meant the world to his grandparents, and Summer couldn't fault them for that. Too, Eloise was basically kind, if rather shallow. She'd been worried about Summer as well as her grandson. She'd wanted to know what Chase's intentions were.

Summer grimaced as she scrubbed off the last of the burned-on lasagna. She hadn't had much of an answer for Eloise. What could she say? That Chase's intentions were purely temporary and involved a lot of mind-blowing sex?

Although his actions the past few days hadn't always agreed with his words.

She shut the water off and reached for the dish towel, her heart aching with hope as much as with the fear she kept pressed down out of sight, during the day.

Hope…because, for a good-time man allergic to responsibility, Chase was acting mighty peculiar.

He kept fixing things. Not things she asked him to work on, either. Yesterday he'd replaced a few missing shingles on Summer's roof. Monday he'd repaired some fencing and tightened the wobbly leg on her kitchen table, and Sunday—after their feast of peanut butter and jelly sandwiches—he'd reorganized the tack room at the stable, getting everything just where he wanted it.

And he hadn't been back to Papa Joe's.

Chase said he would leave her. He gave her no words whatsoever to hang her hope on, but the man too restless to stay in one place hadn't been so far as the bar down the highway since that one time. He did things around the house and stable that, in another person, Summer would have called nest building.

Some corner of her heart, some irrepressibly foolish corner, whispered that maybe it *was* nesting. Maybe Chase was feeling the stirrings of a home hunger his years on the road hadn't managed to kill. And giving up the rodeo meant he had a hole in his life now. Would it be so remarkable if he discovered needs now that he'd never noticed before?

Hope was an uncomfortable guest in Summer's heart, and not entirely welcome. But, like a freeloading relative, hope was impossible to get rid of once it showed up. If she wondered *why* Chase's rodeo days were over, when his knee didn't keep him from riding or training horses, her unwanted guest kept her from giving the question much attention.

Chase thumbed the disconnect and set the phone down slowly. Fear stuck in his throat, a cold, alien lump of feeling he hardly recognized. For years he'd known fear only in brief, exhilarating snatches in the arena, but now...what he felt now wasn't for himself, and that made it worse.

He swallowed, but the lump remained.

According to Henry Gonzales, Ray Fletcher had reason to be desperate. He'd put together a group of investors to capitalize his proposed development. He'd made promises to those investors. But he'd lost his investors a good deal of money on the first site he'd recommended when he'd tried to buy up the land piecemeal and was unable to get a key parcel.

Gonzales had told Chase what Fletcher needed in the land he bought. The land had to be near San Antonio. It had to have water for landscaping and should be near an existing school system, sewage and power lines, and have ready access to the highway. And after the last fiasco, Fletcher needed to find a large block of land to acquire with a single purchase, and he needed to get it cheap—and fast.

Summer's land was perfect. Except she didn't intend to sell.

It had taken some digging, even for a man with Gonzales's resources, to find out who Fletcher's investors were behind the maze of dummy partnerships and paper corporations. But that's what had prompted his call today. Four out of the five people involved had ties to organized crime.

Chase swallowed again, but the fear remained, sullen and foreign.

According to Henry Gonzales, the connection to organized crime didn't have to be a problem. He thought the proposed development was probably a money-laundering setup, and that the underhanded attempts to ruin Summer's business were strictly Fletcher's doing.

The man was probably panicky over what his business associates would do if he were unable to fulfill his promises. The professional criminals, Gonzales claimed, would not be happy to learn Fletcher was operating this way. They liked their money-laundering operations to be squeaky clean.

Unlike Chase, Henry Gonzales was actually pretty cheerful about this aspect of the situation. He promised to drop a word in "the right ear," confident that Fletcher's investors would put a stop to his illegal activities, in order to keep this end of their business aboveboard. No, the problem that had Gonzales worried was much more straightforward.

Summer had been certain the banker she'd dealt with all her life would never sell her loan to Fletcher. Gonzales, accustomed to how loudly the dollar speaks, had decided to check into it himself. He'd heard from a local source, a member of the bank's board of directors, that the bank had received an offer too good to refuse. They were going to sell Summer out.

Chase looked toward the kitchen, where the sound of running water said he had a minute or two to make up his mind about what to tell her. He badly wanted to keep what he'd learned to himself, to spare her any further worry, but this, he decided, couldn't be his call. She had to know…at least, she had to know about Fletcher's ties to organized crime.

Maybe she didn't have to know all of it. Chase was pretty sure he could take care of the problem with the loan. The way he'd have to handle it made him uneasy deep inside, but he'd do it. He'd call his brother that afternoon and get things in motion. This way, he'd be able to offer her a solution in a few days, at the same time she learned about the problem.

It was going to cost him, but he couldn't let Summer lose her land. The land, and her roots here, mattered more to her than anything except her son. And the land would still be here after he was gone.

Ten

The sky was a clear, brilliant blue overhead, though the clouds piling up on the horizon hinted at a chance for yet more rain before the day was over. Summer and Chase were on their way back from the creek, where they'd had a picnic followed by a deliciously illicit dessert.

They were on horseback. Chase had surprised her at lunch with packed saddlebags and a tacked-up Honey-Do and Maverick, whose manners had improved enormously. Summer's hair had started out in a braid, but it hung loose now, with bits of grass tangled in it.

"This was a wonderful idea," she said. Holding the reins in her right hand instead of her left felt awkward, but otherwise it was pure bliss to be on Honey-Do's back again...almost as much bliss as she and Chase had shared on a blanket spread beneath the branches of the oaks and box elders that grew along the creek.

Chase smiled. "That's what you say now. I practically had to kidnap you to get you to knock off work for a couple hours."

"I shouldn't have left everything with Wayne," she said guiltily. Her part-time hand seemed to be working out okay, so she'd asked him to take calls while she was gone—but there were a lot of things he wasn't ready to handle, like most anything to do with the horses. He knew next to nothing about horses.

Yet she'd missed this so much, missed the freedom and exertion and ease of riding. The doctor had wanted her to stay off horseback another week just to be sure, but, she thought, the doctor didn't know how smooth Honey-Do's gait was.

Chase did. He'd understood what the tension of the past several days had been doing to her.

"Wayne can answer the phone if it rings. I don't think that's putting too much of a burden on him," he said dryly. "You just feel guilty about enjoying yourself."

"I'm not used to playing hooky," she admitted. She fell silent, savoring the rhythm of Honey-Do's gait and the easy joy of riding beside Chase. He looked very much the working cowboy today in his old hat and the same jeans and shirt he'd been wearing last Sunday when he taught her new games to play in the stable. She smiled at him. "I guess it doesn't hurt me to take a little time to play once in a while, though."

Chase looked at the glowing woman riding next to him. At least, he thought, he'd done this much right. He'd helped Summer forget her troubles for a while and remember how to play.

Down at the creek, before they both got distracted, she'd talked casually about growing up here, sharing scraps of childhood memories—and giving away maybe more than she realized. "I get the impression," he said, pulling Maverick's nose up when the horse tried to stop and graze, "that your father was pretty old-fashioned. Idle hands and Satan and mischief and all that."

"Well," she said, "he took life pretty seriously. Don't get me wrong—I loved my father, and I'm grateful to him for making sure I had the kind of self-confidence you only get from hard work. I could never have held on to Three Oaks after he died if I hadn't had that to build on. But he was...strict."

"And you rebelled."

"I made us both pretty miserable when I was a teenager. I wanted—oh, all kinds of things he didn't have any use for. Things he thought were just showing off."

"Like barrel racing?" he asked. Summer threw herself into life so wholeheartedly. How could anyone who claimed to love her, he wondered, have tried to suppress that? How could she still feel guilty because she'd fought back? "Was that showing off?"

She looked surprised. "Ricky told you?"

"He said you've got some trophies hiding at the back of your closet."

She looked embarrassed. "Strictly local stuff. Pop wouldn't let me enter anything more than fifty miles away. Of course, when I got married..." She shook her head. "Well, there was never enough money for entry fees then, and when I was at home, Pop thought competing in front of a crowd was nothing but vanity. He didn't trust what he called 'flashy people,' and he warned me about the rodeo crowd often enough. He thought those people were sure to get me in trouble."

She shrugged her good shoulder. "I guess he was right."

"Were you?" he asked quietly.

She glanced at him.

"Were you 'in trouble' when you married Jimmie?" It bothered him, he realized. It bothered him a lot to think of her pregnant by that charming, selfish boy she'd married.

Chase had been running after his rainbow pretty hard in those days, putting mile after mile on his truck, criss-crossing the country in the all-consuming effort to win enough prize money to stay high in the ratings. He'd wanted that Best All-Around title, wanted it bad. And the women…he'd always done pretty well with the ladies, but once he started climbing high in the ratings, he did even better and with less effort. Women came to him then.

The memories didn't sit comfortably with him. He and Jimmie Callaway had wanted the same things seven years ago, hadn't they? The road, the rodeo and the women. Chase had been a little better at the rodeo part of the package than Jimmie, but they just hadn't been all that damned different. Then.

Now Jimmie was dead, and Chase didn't know what the hell he wanted.

Summer's smile was bittersweet. "It might have been better if I had been 'in trouble,' actually. If I'd been pregnant my father would have been disappointed in me, but by then he was disappointed in me all the time, anyway. But a baby—that would have been a reason he could accept for me to marry Jimmie."

"He didn't like Jimmie, I take it." Chase gave her father credit for having at least known a loser when he saw one.

"Lord, no. When I told him Jimmie wanted to marry me, he forbade me to ever see him again." The look on her face said that her memories had turned more bitter than sweet. "Of course, he'd forbidden me all sorts of things that I went ahead and did, from going to movies he didn't approve of to wearing my jeans too tight. I was eighteen, and I knew everything. I was sure that his attitude toward Jimmie was just another way to try and control me."

Chase didn't intend to ask the next question. He didn't think he even wanted to know. Yet it came out. "Did you marry Jimmie because you wanted out from under your father's thumb, or because you were in love with him?"

"Does it have to be just one or the other?"

"Were you in love with him?"

She looked at him, then stood in the stirrups, arching her lower back, stretching muscles that, after three weeks away from riding, were probably stiffening. The motion was incredibly sensual, and he started to harden in spite of what they'd done with each other down by the creek. "Yes," she said at last, her eyes unfocused as if she were looking into the past. "I was in love. Maybe there were other motives mixed in, and maybe it wasn't the forever-after kind of feeling I thought it was, but I did love Jimmie once."

Chase wanted to hit something. A dead man, maybe, as stupid as that might be. Maverick picked up his rider's tension and jittered sideways.

Summer glanced at him, licked her lips and asked, "What about you, Chase? Have you ever been in love?"

"No." He knew what she was really asking. He

knew how he had to answer, and his voice was hard when he did. "No, I've never been in love."

She didn't speak again.

They passed through the gate that opened onto the main yard, and had circled the kennel before they saw the car, an aging four-door sedan, pulled up next to the house. Chase thought someone was sitting inside, though the angle of the sun created too much glare on the windshield for him to see clearly. He frowned.

"Oh, shi—I mean, shoot," Summer said, as the car door opened. "Chase—I hate to ask, but could you let Wayne know we're back, and then take care of Honey-Do? That's my mother-in-law."

Jimmie's mother. As their horses ambled to a stop at the hitching rail, Chase watched a plump, older woman in a pink gingham dress climb out of the car. Rick had stayed after school with his grandparents a couple times since Chase's arrival, but both times Summer had gone into town to pick him up after supper, so Chase hadn't seen the woman before. He wondered what brought her here today.

Him, maybe?

He glanced at Summer. Ricky's grandmother was a permanent part of their lives. He wasn't. "No problem," he said, swinging down from Maverick. "I'll stay in the stable while she's here."

She didn't have to tilt her chin up much to look down her nose at him when she was on horseback and he was afoot. "What if I don't want that? What if I ask you to come in and meet her?"

He clipped the lead rope looped around the hitching rail to Maverick's halter. "We don't always get what we want, do we, sugar?"

When she swung down from Honey-Do's back, she wouldn't let him help her. He wasn't surprised.

Summer carried the saddlebags that held the remains of their picnic as she walked stiffly across the yard to where Eloise Callaway waited. She was getting pretty sick of how hard Chase worked at keeping his distance. And she hated it when he called her "sugar."

Eloise waited by her car for Summer. The heels she wore with her pink-and-white checked dress might get soiled crossing the hazardous territory of a stable yard, after all. Besides, as Summer knew very well, the older woman considered her age and her status as Jimmie's mother sufficient that Summer should always be the one to come to her.

"I hope you haven't been waiting long, Eloise," Summer said when she reached her. "I apologize for smelling like my horse. I certainly wouldn't have gone riding if I'd known you were coming."

"I'm sure you wouldn't," the other woman said, as if this were proof of misbehavior on Summer's part. "I've heard—oh, my, such unpleasant news, Summer, and I came straight out so we could talk."

Summer had always felt awkward around Jimmie's mother, who was her opposite in so many ways. Eloise thought that ladies wore heels and dresses. She considered pink the only decent color for lipstick, red being too gaudy. Judging from the way the woman was pursing her Pink Sherbet lips right now, Summer had the feeling she wasn't going to enjoy their talk. "Let's go inside, then. Would you rather have coffee or iced tea?"

"Neither," Eloise said. She darted a nervous glance at the barn. "Is that…him?"

It was going to be one of *those* conversations, was

it? "If you're asking whether the man I rode in with is Chase McGuire, the answer is yes."

"Summer." Eloise surprised her by reaching out and gripping her arm. "What do you really know about that man?"

Summer's eyebrows went up. "What is it you want to know?"

"Does he have a brother? A brother with a ranch up in Alaska or Montana or someplace north like that?"

Summer managed not to smile. To Eloise, who'd lived in Bita Creek all fifty-seven years of her life, all those states "up north" were pretty interchangeable. "Wyoming?" she suggested, wondering how in the world the small-town grapevine had managed to pick up on that bit of information.

Eloise dropped her hand. She looked truly distressed. "You've got to put an end to this—this—whatever your relationship is with him. It just won't do. I understand your feelings. He, well, he is rather a fine-looking man—" the older woman turned pink at this delicate reference to Chase's body "—and you've been alone for some time, but you have a young son. You have to think of Ricky first."

"I always have." Summer paused to smooth out the edge that temper put on her voice. "Look, Eloise, let's either drop the subject or go in, sit down and talk this out."

Eloise shook her head. Her pale gray and pale brown hairs didn't sway with the movement. At her standing Friday-afternoon appointment at Cut 'n' Curl, Thelma glued everything in place firmly enough to last until the next Friday. "I just want your promise, Summer. Promise me you won't take Ricky with you. He can stay

with Ed and me. That would be best, you know—a boy
his age can't be traveling on the road all the time.''

"Take Ricky with me?" Summer repeated, bewildered.

"You can't take him away," the other woman said,
her voice rising, agitated color flooding her face. "He's
all that Ed and I have left of Jimmie."

This time Summer was the one to reach out and touch
the other woman's arm. "Eloise, I don't know what
you're talking about. Calm down."

Eloise bit her lip. "All right. Maybe I'm jumping to
conclusions. It's just…" Her plump breasts heaved
with a sigh. "When Lillian over at the bank told me,
all I could think of was that you must be planning to
go off with this cowboy of yours, and I couldn't stand
it."

Alarm prickled down Summer's spine. "What did
Lillian at the bank tell you?"

"About you selling the stable. You've always trea-
sured this land. You wouldn't sell it unless you were
planning to—to go away and not come back." She
blinked rapidly to clear the tears filming her eyes.

Summer breathed a sigh of relief. Obviously the rumor mill had gone a little wild with this particular story.
"Lillian has her facts wrong this time. I'm not selling
anything."

"But she said—she saw the papers, Summer. About
the loan."

Loan?

"The papers that brother up north sent about assum-
ing the loan on your place. They had his name on it,
and your cowboy's name, too. It's because you're selling, isn't it? To that brother of his?"

For one blind, bewildered minute Summer couldn't

get her breath. Then it came rushing in, along with the reality of loss. For the next few minutes she mechanically soothed her mother-in-law, promising that she really, truly wasn't going anywhere. She was numb, her mind too sluggish to sort out exactly what she'd lost just now—but something was definitely gone, something vast and necessary, something whose absence left her hollow and uncertain.

As soon as she'd closed the big gate behind Eloise's departing Buick, she turned and stared at the stable. Chase was there. Chase, whose brother had bought the loan on Summer's land.

Slowly she started for the stable.

She must have walked from bright sunlight to the stable's dimness thousands of times in her life. In June or July the shade beneath the stable's roof would welcome her; in winter the animals' warmth made the building cozy and inviting.

Today she felt nothing at all as she moved from light to shadow.

Chase was just closing Honey-Do's stall. Maverick was already shut up in his, she noticed dispassionately. Chase must have really hurried to get both horses untacked and groomed so quickly.

"Wayne's not here," he said when he saw her walking toward him. "I guess he's over at the kennel. Is your mother-in-law gone? I heard a car."

"Oh, she's gone. But you should have overcome your scruples about meeting her, Chase. Maybe you could have kept her from giving away so much."

His brows pulled down. "What are you talking about?"

"Secrets." Abruptly she couldn't look at him anymore. She walked on past him, then turned around.

Maybe, she thought, Eloise was wrong. Maybe she had everything wrong. Summer stood stiffly and asked, "Has your brother bought my loan from the bank?"

He didn't even have to answer. She saw it in his eyes, the quick, guilty slide away, then back. "Not exactly."

"Not exactly?" Somewhere deep inside was a frantic creature clawing at her gut, but outside she stayed calm. Frozen. "What does that mean?"

"It means that I bought the note, not my brother."

Chase? Chase, who had no money, no assets beyond a few trophy buckles and a broken truck—Chase bought a note that had a balance of nearly twenty thousand dollars? If she'd been shocked before, she was truly stunned now.

"Look, I know I should have said something." He took a step toward her.

She took a step back.

"Okay, you're upset." He ran a hand over his hair. "I was going to tell you tomorrow. I just heard from the bank this morning that the papers are all in and ready for me to sign. I was waiting until everything was done so that you wouldn't worry. I know you've been worrying. I thought I could help."

"Help?" Her voice came out unnaturally high. "You thought that would help?"

"I didn't tell you everything Henry Gonzales said when he called last week. Fletcher had made an offer to your bank to purchase several notes—he'd made them a package deal in order to get hold of yours. The bank was going to end up taking the offer. It was too damned good to pass up. But your banker managed to stall things long enough for me to set up an alternative."

"Chase," she said as slowly and patiently as if he

were the one needing explanations, "how could you buy my loan from the bank? How could you begin to have that kind of money? You're working here for little better than minimum wage. You didn't have enough money to fix your truck."

"The money's mine," he said, looking uncomfortable, "technically. My brother's been paying it into an account in my name ever since Jennifer was born and needed all that extra care—though just a little at first. The ranch wasn't making much in those days because he was still paying off the loan he took out to buy a good-size piece of land shortly before he got married."

Slowly, terribly, her mind began to grasp what it was that she had lost. "He's been paying you back."

Chase nodded. "I told him it was damned stupid, that ranching is enough of a gamble without him siphoning off that kind of money, but he never listens to me. He said if I kept trying to give it back or put it in trust for Jennifer or something, he'd sign the other half of the ranch over to me." Chase stopped and rubbed the back of his neck, embarrassed. "Well, I could have kept arguing, but in the end we agreed that the money could go into an account in both our names. He can use it for Jenny's therapy or medical care, and I—I hadn't intended to use it at all, but I couldn't let you lose your land."

Summer closed her eyes, shutting him out while she tried to hold herself together in spite of what she'd lost.

Hope. With hope gone, the sight of him hurt her heart. "The 'other half of the ranch.' You own half your brother's ranch."

"Half of the original ranch, but only technically." He moved toward her. "My parents left the ranch to both of us, but it's not really mine. Mike's the one who put his blood and sweat into the operation. I guess I should have told you about Fletcher trying to take over the note, but I wanted to wait until I knew if my solution would work.'' He reached for her.

"Don't touch me.'' She heard and despised the hysterical note in her voice. "I don't know you at all, do I? How much money do you have?''

He frowned. "It isn't mine. Not really. I haven't deceived you, Summer. I really did need this job.''

"Did you? So that you didn't have to use the money that isn't yours—just like your share of the ranch isn't really yours?'' He said he hadn't lied, but omitting a truth this large felt like a lie. "Oh, I understand, all right, Chase. As long as none of it's really yours, you don't have to be responsible for it, do you? And that's the whole point.''

He moved faster than her, grabbing her by the waist before she could get away. "The point,'' he said grimly, "is that I tapped into money I'd never intended to touch, so you wouldn't lose your land.''

"No,'' she said, shaking her head so hard her hair flew out, tangling around his hand on her shoulder. "Oh, no. The point is that, in a sense, we're owned by the things we own. You won't let yourself be tied down, not to your brother, not to a ranch—not even to a bank account, for God's sake, much less a woman who—oh, God,'' she said, as tears threatened. "I've been such a fool.''

His hands fell away. She could see the doors slamming behind his eyes. And unasked, unwilled, the wild, frantic thing inside her fluttered out: "I love you.''

He stood there and looked at her out of eyes so flat he couldn't possibly have seen her, and he didn't say anything at all.

She closed her eyes, trying to climb over the pain. "This is your chance to say 'I told you so,' isn't it?" She'd had it all wrong. She'd thought all the things he'd been doing meant that deep down he wanted a place to belong. A home. But he'd done those things for her, not himself. Chase gave freely, generously, to those he cared about because it was easier for him to give than to take. Giving let him stay free.

Nothing—not even pity—moved in his eyes when he said, "I'll be moving on as soon as I can check with Gonzales and make sure Fletcher can't pull any more tricks. Tomorrow, probably."

She felt dizzy and cold. Pride kept her chin up, but she didn't know what made her voice sound so cool, so detached. "I'll have your check ready," she told him. And, because she couldn't help herself, she asked, "Where will you go? Your truck isn't ready. You don't…" *Have enough money to pay for it yet,* she almost said.

"I gave the garage a down payment on the motor last week. I'll either keep paying it out, or—" He grimaced, and for the first time something flickered in his eyes, but she couldn't tell what it was. The ice surrounding her was too isolating.

"You should be out of the woods," he said, "with Fletcher. I'll check with Gonzales to make sure, but with his associates putting pressure on him to stay within the law, and with this last effort of his falling flat, you ought to be all right. As for the loan, you can pay that back however you want."

"You can't have it." She stood tall in the chilly ashes of her pride. "You can't have the note, Chase."

"You don't have any choice."

"I'll take out another loan elsewhere and pay you back."

"Dammit, woman, are you crazy? That's an open invitation to Fletcher to step in. He'll just buy it and call it due!"

"That's not your problem, is it? You won't be here. You'll have moved on down the road, just as free as ever." She started to turn away.

His hand stopped her, swinging her back to face him so abruptly she staggered slightly. If he'd been impossible to read before, she had no doubt what he felt now.

Anger. It radiated from his tense body, blazed from his eyes, throbbed in his voice. "This was what you wanted, Summer. No," he said, his fingers digging into her arm when she tried to pull away, "I'm not going to let you go back and hide in your cozy little house, wrapped up all snug and proud in your precious independence and blaming me for doing what I said all along I'd do. What you wanted me to do."

"I never wanted you to leave!" she cried, stung.

"Oh, yes, you did. You know how to be alone, and you'd rather hang on to what you know, even if it hurts. You never asked me to stay. Hell, you never invited me into your bed, or even your bedroom. You always came to me—and then you left. Every time. You haven't asked me for one damned thing, and having to take something from me now in order to hang on to your land is practically choking you."

She shook her head mutely. He was wrong. He must be wrong. She hadn't asked him to stay because he didn't want her to ask.

His face was grim. "No more hiding, Summer. You wanted the leaving as well as the loving. If you'd been a different kind of woman you'd have had a fling with a married man, someone who couldn't expect much from you, but you couldn't handle that. Someone like me, someone who wasn't going to stay, was the next best thing.''

He'd stripped her bare of her defenses. She stood in front of him, empty of hope and words. Any words. Though she desperately wanted to argue with him, she had no words.

Once more he dropped his hand, leaving her arm throbbing where his fingers had bitten into the flesh. ''Don't let your pride cheat you out of what matters, Summer,'' he said quietly. ''Keep the loan, even if it means keeping a tie with me. Keep your land.''

Numbly she turned away, and this time he let her. She paused at the doorway without looking back. ''Ricky will be home in half an hour. I'll break the news to him, but you should be prepared for him to come rushing over to try and talk you out of leaving. Children don't understand that sort of thing.''

His silence lasted several heartbeats this time. ''I know,'' he said at last, sounding tired and sad.

Summer managed to walk across the yard with her shoulders squared, her stride steady and her back to him, so that he wouldn't see her tears.

Eleven

Slowly Summer scraped corn, potatoes and leftover roast from the untouched plate into the trash. It was 9:12 and Ricky was in bed, though maybe not asleep. Her son had gone to see Chase right after school. Right after she told him Chase was leaving. But he'd come back all too soon, and he'd spent most of the time since closed up in his room.

Ricky had said Chase wasn't going to eat with them, but she'd saved him a plate, anyway. Just in case.

He hadn't come.

You could make him stay if you wanted to.

Ricky had said that to her when she told him Chase was leaving. He'd said it again when he went to bed. She'd tried to explain that Chase was an adult who made his own decisions, but Ricky was young enough to want his mother to be able to fix anything. He'd been angry—with her, with his hero, with the world. When she tucked him in, he hadn't let her hug him. When she bent to kiss him good-night, he'd turned his face away.

But that, she thought wearily as she rinsed the plate and stacked it in the dishwasher, hadn't been just because he was mad. His eyes had been shiny with tears, and he hadn't wanted her to see. In the past year her little boy had decided that only sissies cried.

Summer took a clean sponge and wiped down the table, washing away the last traces of a meal neither she nor Ricky had eaten much of.

You could make him stay....

"How?" she whispered to her spotless kitchen.

A knock sounded at the back door. She dropped the sponge.

Because Hannah hadn't barked, Summer didn't check the peephole before opening the door. He wore expensive black boots, a black Stetson with silver conchas, and an emerald green shirt. She swallowed.

It looked like Chase was going somewhere tonight.

He didn't come all the way up to the door, but hung back in the shadows. "Do you mind if I use your truck to go into town?"

She wanted to tell him to walk. She wanted to ask where he was going and why, and she wondered, sickly, if he could go from her to another woman this quickly. Surely not. Surely he couldn't ask to use her truck if he wanted to go into town for *that.*

She wanted to ask him to stay. And couldn't. "Go ahead," she told him.

After he nodded and left, after she closed the door and stood there in her bright, empty kitchen, she heard her words over and over. *Go ahead.* As if she were giving him permission to leave. Why hadn't she told him no, he couldn't use her truck without telling her

why he needed it? Why hadn't she asked him to stay—
tonight, tomorrow, forever—instead of saying blankly
go ahead?

Those questions led to others. Why hadn't she let the
man she'd allowed into her heart and her body into her
bed? She'd gone to his bed eagerly enough, but he was
right—she'd never asked him to come to her. She
wanted to think it was because of Ricky. Oh, she did
want to think that, but she'd never made a conscious
decision to keep her relationship with Chase a secret
from her son.

Chase had never seen her bedroom. He knew her
body intimately, but he'd never seen her bedroom.

He was wrong about her wanting him to leave.
Wasn't he?

The phone rang twice before Summer noticed and
pulled herself together enough to answer. It must have
been a wrong number, though. They hung up as soon
as she said hello.

Papa Joe's didn't improve on closer acquaintance.
One of the customers tonight was a Tammy Wynette
fan, apparently, since this was the third time Chase had
scowled through "Stand by Your Man." The place still
smelled of cigarettes and stale beer, and the customers
looked more interested in drinking than in each other.
But then, no one came to a joint like Papa Joe's on a
Monday night if they had someplace better to be.

Chase took a long drink of the beer the bartender set
in front of him and tried to persuade himself that his
reason for being there made a difference, that he wasn't
as pathetic as the rest of the jokers clumped up around
the bar or the pool tables.

He didn't succeed.

Chase had come into town because he wanted to make sure Summer's part-time hand would be able to work for her full-time, starting tomorrow. When he didn't find Wayne at the boarding house, he'd come to Papa Joe's, knowing Wayne hung out here a lot. Two hours and two beers later, he was wondering if it was time to admit he wasn't going to find the man tonight. Of course, if he did admit that, he'd have no excuse to stay away from the kennel with its small, dreary room and the narrow bed where he'd made love to Summer over and over.

No way would he be able to sleep in that bed tonight.

He shouldn't have said those things to her. Oh, he'd been right. On some level she'd recognized the truth when she heard it, too, but what difference did that make? Why hadn't he let her go on believing the things she told herself? They were mostly true, even if they weren't the whole truth.

"Mr. McGuire?" said an uncertain voice behind him.

He knew that voice. Chase swiveled on his stool. "You've got one hell of a nerve coming up to me, Raul. I've been wanting a chance to explain my opinion of you. Preferably someplace nice and private." Chase looked the boy over and wondered if he had enough conscience left to keep him from teaching Raul a lesson.

Raul was a head shorter than Chase and twenty or thirty pounds of muscle heavier, but it didn't look like he doubted Chase's ability to follow through on his "explanation." His Adam's apple bobbed when he swallowed. "I know I was wrong. I shouldn't have done it, but the money—man, I needed that money."

Chase's hands curled into fists. "And that makes it okay to poison animals?"

"I didn't! I wouldn't have given them the bad hay, not ever. And I knew she wouldn't. She loves those animals. But I got to talk to you, man. I couldn't tell her," he said. "I called, but I just couldn't speak to her after—after everything. Then I saw you in here, and I thought, if I tell him, he can handle it."

Chase's senses came on full alert. "Tell who? Summer? What couldn't you tell her?"

"Hey," the bartender said gruffly. "Get outa here, kid. You know you got to stay in the other room, away from the bar."

Chase stood, looking down at Raul. "Let's step outside," he said. "And talk."

The night was damp and chilly. Clouds had moved in to cover the moon and stars, and the wind blew in erratic fits and starts. The stable light wasn't enough to soften the darkness that lay between the house and the kennel, not in the eyes of a seven-year-old boy who'd never snuck outside alone at night before.

But Ricky was his mother's son. Once he set his mind on something, he did it.

Besides, he had Kelpie with him. Ricky ran his hand over the dog's head for reassurance.

It was hard to say things right. He was miserably aware he hadn't said anything right when Chase told him about how he was leaving. He'd gotten mad, and he never said things the way he needed to when he was mad. Then he'd had to leave because he was going to cry. If Chase saw him crying he'd think Ricky was just a dumb little kid who cried when he couldn't get what he wanted.

Ricky sure hoped the letter he'd written after supper said things right. He'd spent a long time on it, but he didn't know that many words, and a lot of the ones he did know, he couldn't spell. He just knew he didn't want Chase to go. He figured Chase must be pretty mad to want to leave so quickly, either mad at him or at his mom, so he'd said ''sorry'' for both of them in his letter.

Then he'd lain awake in bed and worried. What if he missed Chase in the morning? That was too awful to think about, so he'd slipped out of bed while his mom was in her room. The key to the kennel hung on a hook by the back door, so he'd brought it with him. He was going to leave the letter on Chase's chest of drawers, right by the buckle and the framed photograph. Chase couldn't miss seeing it there.

He was less than halfway across the yard when Kelpie gave a little yip and ran off toward the stable. Ricky called her, but the stupid dog didn't come. She just went off and left him there.

He stared after her, trying to make up his mind to go on to the kennel by himself.

Something was different at the stable. He frowned. Something was wrong. He couldn't figure out what, though. Kelpie hadn't acted upset. She'd gone running off as if she were racing to greet a friend. 'Course, the stupid dog thought everyone was her friend.

Drawn by both the powerful curiosity of the young and his desire for his dog's company, Ricky started for the stable.

At 11:13 Summer was still awake. She wasn't even in bed, though she'd gone into her room and put her nightgown on a few minutes ago, leaving her sling off.

She was standing in the darkened living room, coming to terms with some unpleasant truths about herself, when Hannah's deep bray sounded from the back porch.

Alarm shot her to her feet. She hurried to the hall as the kennel dogs joined Hannah. When she didn't see Ricky standing in his doorway, blinking sleepily and demanding to know what was happening, she breathed a sigh of relief. Thank heavens he was such a sound sleeper. She dashed into her room, pulled on the robe that went with her nightgown—the same gown and robe she'd worn the first night she went to Chase—grabbed a small key from her jewelry box, and hurried back to the living room.

There, she unlocked the gun cabinet. She hesitated briefly between the .22 and her father's old Remington shotgun. The .22 was good for snakes, but she didn't think any snake had woken Hannah in the middle of the night. The load she had for the shotgun was rock salt, not buckshot. Summer had never been able to aim at anything to kill, and rock salt burned plenty bad enough to discourage a skunk or feral dog.

She might have a human target tonight.

Summer took down the shotgun and grabbed a couple of the custom-loaded cartridges. If she had trouble shooting at a wild dog, she didn't expect she'd be able to pull the trigger on a man.

As soon as she stepped out on the porch, Hannah quieted. The dogs at the kennel were still making enough commotion that it took a minute before she realized Kelpie's excited yips were coming from the stable. She frowned. Kelpie, unlike Hannah, was perfectly capable of getting worked up over anything from a stray cat to a leaf drifting in the wind.

But Hannah, though she wasn't baying, wasn't settling down, either. She came over to Summer, snuffling against her hand, still stirred up—and watching the stable.

"Okay, sweetie," Summer whispered, laying her hand on the old dog's head. "I'll take it from here." She took a deep breath, checked the safety, and breached a cartridge. The distinctive *snick-snack* of a shotgun ready to fire sounded clear and ominous. She started across the yard to the stable with the heavy gun pointed at the ground, ready to raise to her good shoulder. Thunder rumbled overhead, and a fretful wind tugged at the full skirts of her gown and robe.

She was halfway to the stable when something thumped loudly against the wall of the barn. She stopped, her heart pounding. It was a moment before she realized what had made the noise, and when she did, her alarm increased.

The gate between the inside and outside portions of one of the stalls hung open. Even as she watched, the wind flung it against the barn again.

All the outside gates should have been closed. Anytime bad weather threatened, she made sure those gates were closed.

She took a deep breath to steady herself and started toward the dark, gaping hole that was the doorway to the stable. Wearing white like she was, she'd be easily visible to anyone inside the stable. The light switch was just inside the doorway, though. If she could flip that on quickly, she ought to have the advantage of... whoever.

Summer's truck shook like a palsied old man when Chase got it up to eighty-two and held it there, praying for more speed with every breath that didn't curse himself, Ray Fletcher or Raul.

Dammit, why hadn't the kid spoken up earlier? Why had he waited so late to decide he couldn't live with himself if he stayed silent? Chase kept the shimmying truck pointed straight down the highway and reminded himself that he didn't know for certain that anything was wrong at Three Oaks. Yeah, Wayne was probably a plant, but that wasn't proof that something was going down *tonight*.

Fletcher had approached Raul again after Chase discovered the moldy hay. He'd wanted to know if Raul could get into the stable easily at night to take care of "another little job." Raul had turned him down. Two days later Wayne had shown up, looking for a job. Now, eleven days after the fact, Raul had decided that Fletcher must have something really nasty in mind.

And Chase hadn't been able to find Wayne.

All he had were guesses. Chase told himself that, but he knew better. Fate had been saving up for tonight, and now, while he was away, something terrible was happening. Something he might have prevented if he hadn't gone looking for Wayne—looking for a way to keep from going to Summer tonight and begging for one last time together.

He cursed again as he took the final curve of the highway before it went past Summer's place. The truck skidded across the center line. Twin headlights warned of an oncoming car, and the blare of a horn sounded even as Chase wrenched the truck back into his own lane.

When he slammed on the brakes a minute later and the truck shuddered to a stop outside the smaller gate, the house was dark—but the stable wasn't.

Chase was out of the truck and moving in two heart-pounding seconds. Some of the kennel dogs were barking, and he counted on their racket to mask the noise he made. He circled to the north end of the stable, away from the house, where there was more cover, more shadows. His mouth was dry, his feet sure and silent as he edged along the rough wooden exterior of the building. Wayne might well be armed, and he wanted every second of surprise he could get.

But what he saw when he peered around the corner of the northern doorway froze the blood in his veins.

Summer. At the other end of the stable in her long white nightgown and robe. The shotgun braced against her shoulder was pointed at Wayne...who held a knife to her son's throat.

Kelpie sat by Summer's left foot, panting nervously. The dog wasn't good at being still, and the command to *sit* made her unhappy. Overhead, the fluorescent light Summer had switched on seconds or eons ago hummed noisily. One of the horses shifted sleepily in its stall. Summer's throat hurt from the purest terror she'd ever known, and her bad shoulder already ached from keeping the shotgun up and pointed.

Ten feet away from the business end of the twin barrels a man held her son. A man she'd hired. A grinning, red-haired man who'd had references, who should have been safe. Next to his feet sat a can of gasoline. "Looks like we've got us a problem, don't it, Miz Callaway?" Wayne said mildly.

Wayne wasn't a tall man, not much taller than her. He had freckles on the forearm hooked under Ricky's chin. He was a good worker, and he was left-handed.

He held the knife in his left hand.

Ricky's face was white with terror. His eyes—God, she couldn't stand to look at his eyes. She kept her gun pointed at Wayne's head, but it was pure bluff. Without real shot in the barrels, she couldn't take the chance of firing. She could hit him square in the face, and even rock salt would do a lot of damage at this range—but she wouldn't kill him.

And Summer, who hadn't thought she could shoot at a skunk to kill, wouldn't hesitate to kill this man if she had the chance. "Let go of my son," she said. "Let go of him, and I'll let you get away."

He shook his head. "Now, you know I can't do that. But I really don't want to hurt the boy. People get all bent out of shape when a kid gets hurt, and that could be a problem for me, and not one I'd planned on when I took this job. So if you and I can work things out so that your boy doesn't get hurt, why, I'd be just as pleased as could be."

She swallowed. It was important, vitally important, that she not let her terror get the better of her. "All you have to do is leave."

"But I'm not finished. 'A workman is worthy of his hire,' you know, and I haven't finished what I was hired to do." Ricky squirmed. Wayne's good-natured mask slipped. "Be still, kid," he growled, his arm tightening around Ricky's throat. "Real still."

"It'll be okay," Summer told Ricky softly through the haze of fear and rage. "Be quiet like he says, and we'll work everything out."

Wayne turned cheerful again. "Good advice, Mom," he said. "You'll do like I say, too, won't you? See, I'm going to burn down your stable, and you're going to help."

Summer opened her mouth to answer but nothing

came out. Nothing—not a word—formed in her suddenly blank mind, because forty feet behind Wayne, Chase McGuire had slipped inside the stable.

She blinked and scrambled for control. "I—I—" She swallowed as Chase took one slow, silent step toward the man whose back was—mostly—to him. Chase's eyes met hers. His expression was neither fierce nor frightened. Just *focused,* absolutely focused. Like when he trained horses. Probably the way he'd looked when he'd climbed on the back of a bronc or a bull.

Something resembling the quiet at the eye of the storm invaded her during that flickering second of contact. If she could keep Wayne occupied, keep his attention on her, Chase would take the man out. He'd do it so that Ricky wasn't hurt. She knew that, knew it surely enough that for the first time since she'd turned on the light in the stable and seen Wayne holding her son, she was almost calm.

"What do you want me to do?" she asked the man with the knife.

He chuckled. "Well, for starters, you'd better put that gun down."

"But if I put it down," she said, "I lose my bargaining power, don't I?"

Chase was three steps closer.

"Well, ma'am, the fact is, you don't have any bargaining power. See, I don't have to kill the boy. All I have to do—" he moved the knife so quickly she barely followed the flick of the blade from vulnerable throat to skinny chest and back "—is hurt him a bit."

When Ricky cried out, Summer almost squeezed the trigger. But the knife hadn't sliced anything more important than the waffle-weave of his pajamas, which hung open now, showing her the unmarked skin of his chest.

"I'm good with a blade," Wayne said, "good enough that I can pretty much do what I want without losing any of my own bargaining power. But you're stuck with only two choices. You can shoot me, or you can put that gun down. Which is it gonna be?" He grinned.

Summer wanted to shoot. She wanted it so badly she shook. But she couldn't. Slowly, painfully slowly, she lowered the gun from her shoulder.

Twenty feet behind Wayne, Chase nodded his head slightly. And took another step forward, drawing abreast of Maverick's stall.

"Ricky," she said, "it's going to be all right. I promise you. Everything will be all right."

Maverick whickered, and stretched his nose out to the man he'd come to like. And at Summer's feet, Kelpie forgot about minding. If anyone was going to get attention, she wanted it to be her. She got to her feet and trotted toward Chase, tail wagging.

Wayne frowned. His gaze shifted, and his head started to turn to follow the dog.

"All right," Summer said quickly as she bent to set the shotgun down. "All right, I'm putting the safety on, okay? I don't want it going off and shooting me or something."

"Gun safety? Good for you, Mom. Set the boy an example." Good humor restored by his wit and her helplessness, Wayne chuckled and forgot about Kelpie, who stopped in front of Chase, tail still wagging. "Now, come on over here. I was just getting down to business, see, when this curious boy of yours came along. So you can help me finish. Take that can of gasoline and pour some over the wood of this next stall.'' He nodded at the stall where a sleepy, placid Honey-Do watched them with mild interest.

''The horses.'' Her brain went stupid on her, and for a moment her legs wouldn't work, either. ''You want me to burn my horses.''

Chase was easing around Kelpie's happily wiggling body.

''Hey, I'm not into wanton violence,'' Wayne said. ''No, ma'am. Besides, no one would believe you set fire to the stable if your horses got turned into crispy critters, so that wouldn't do. See, my employer wants you to be blamed. That way there's no insurance money. That's why I went around and opened the outside gates first—so the horses can get out of the burning building. It's just the sort of thing an animal lover like you would do, isn't it?'' He looked pleased with himself.

Chase was twelve feet away. Kelpie was following him.

''Come on, now, do as you're told,'' Wayne said impatiently. ''This is working out pretty good. Your fingerprints will be all over that gas can now.''

Summer stepped forward. ''But I'll tell them I was forced to do this.'' Another step, her eyes fixed on Wayne's smiling face, her attention fixed on the man who crept silently closer.

''Maybe they'll believe you, maybe they won't.'' He didn't look worried.

He meant to kill them. She was suddenly sure of that. He wasn't worried, because he intended to kill them. Involuntarily her eyes shifted to Chase's face.

Chase wouldn't let Wayne hurt them. If she could hold herself together a little longer, Chase would do what had to be done. She didn't know how he was going to get that knife away from Ricky's throat, but she knew he would. If she just held herself together long enough.

He was about eight feet behind Wayne now—so close, but all Wayne had to do was turn his head and see him, and Chase would be as trapped by the knife at Ricky's throat as she was.

She had to keep Wayne from hearing Chase, only seven feet back.

"I guess Fletcher's the one paying you," she said as she walked toward Wayne, her son and the gas can. *Six feet.* "He won't like it if you kill me, you know. Do you have any idea how much trouble it is in Texas to get an estate cleared up if a person dies without a will?" *Five feet.* "He needs this land a lot quicker than that. So if that's what you have in mind—" she'd reached the gas can and paused to smile reassuringly at Ricky before bending "—you'd better come up with—"

Chase sprang.

His target was Wayne's arm. He connected, knocking the arm, holding the knife away from Ricky, even as the two men tumbled to the dirt floor together—while Summer lunged for Ricky, grabbed him and dropped and rolled the two of them several feet away.

At first she could only huddle there, shaking, her body protecting her son's, barely aware of the sounds of struggle only a few feet away. Her collarbone throbbed, but she didn't care if she'd broken it all over again.

"Mom," Ricky's voice said, muffled, from the region of her chest. "Mom, I'm OK."

She held on fiercely one more second. Then she hauled both of them to their feet, placing herself between him and the men brawling a few feet away. "Get the shotgun," she told him, and made herself let go of him.

Summer had seen high school boys fight. She'd seen a few bar fights in her days of traveling the circuit. But she'd never seen two men fighting for their lives. It was quick and vicious and ugly—and Wayne was the one with the knife.

The fight upset Kelpie, who darted around the men, yelping and getting in the way. Summer grabbed the dog's collar and jerked her back.

The two men rolled. Summer heard one of them cry out and saw a long, red line drawn along Chase's arm. It immediately overflowed with rich, shiny blood. Her mouth went dry with horror. She hadn't even seen the knife cut him—

"Mom!" Ricky said from behind her.

She turned, released Kelpie and grabbed the shotgun. "Get to the phone," she said. There was an extension at the south end of the stable. "Call 911 and stay back."

Ricky ran. Summer turned, clicking off the safety. Her collarbone ached, but she lifted the weapon.

She couldn't get close. The two men rolled and grunted and cursed and kicked until Chase's blood smeared them both, and she couldn't get a clear shot. Not until they rolled right to her feet, nearly knocking her over, with Wayne ending up on top—his hand at Chase's throat, his other arm drawing back, under-handed, for a gut-stabbing—

Fresh terror swamped her, but she didn't hesitate. She pressed both barrels of the shotgun hard against the red-haired man's cheek. "I'm shaking pretty bad," she said, and her voice shook, too. "I don't think you want to startle me right now."

Silence, except for the rasp of both men's breath. Stillness. Finally Wayne said, "No, ma'am, I guess I don't." And slowly, carefully, he laid the knife down.

Twelve

Every man Summer saw that night felt obliged to tell her what an idiot she was for going after a prowler with a gun loaded with rock salt. From the sheriff's deputy who got there first, to the paramedics who came out with the ambulance, to the three neighbors who came and took over the job of resettling the horses and clearing away the blood-soaked soil inside the stable, they all had something to say on the subject. Even the sheriff, who arrived while the ambulance's cherry red light strobed the darkness outside the stable, took the time to tell her what she should have done differently.

Every man, except for the wounded one the paramedics took away in their ambulance.

"It wouldn't have made any difference," she said wearily to Sheriff Potts. The two of them were in the living room. Ricky was in bed, carried there after falling asleep with his head in her lap while officialdom went about its slow business. "Maybe I would have taken a chance on firing when he held Ricky if I'd had the .22 instead of the shotgun. Maybe not."

"Well," Sheriff Potts said, "I guess that's true. And it wouldn't have mattered what your load was when the two men were scrapping. You had to wait until you could get the barrels right up against that bastard's head, and even rock salt would have killed him if you'd pulled the trigger then."

Summer remembered Chase's blood covering his arm and chest, Wayne's arm drawn back, the knife gripped for a thrust—and shuddered.

The sheriff reached out and gave her a kindly pat on her left arm, which once more rested in the sling. "You sure I shouldn't give Aunt Maud a holler?" Potts was one of Maud's nephews. "She'd be over in a flash to keep you company."

Summer wrapped her right arm around her middle and shook her head. "Later, maybe." When she went into town to see Chase at the hospital, she might see if Maud would stay here with Ricky. Chase had tried to dig in his heels about the hospital, of course, but even a rough, tough rodeo cowboy couldn't very well stitch up his own arm.

She hadn't been able to ride in the ambulance with him. Ricky had needed her here.

Summer managed to smile at the sheriff. "No offense, but right now I just want to get the lot of you cleared out so I can be by myself a bit."

Sheriff Potts delayed, however, until he got a phone call telling him that the San Antonio police had Fletcher in custody. "Bail can be delayed for a bit while we get Wayne Redringer's testimony to them," he told her, satisfied. "You won't need to worry about him getting out and bothering you."

Summer had wanted everyone gone, but as soon as the door closed behind the sheriff she changed her mind. Fear pressed in along with solitude and the 3:00 a.m. darkness. Yet there was relief in being at last alone. She could go ahead and fall apart.

Her collapse was quiet. She sat on the couch, wrapped up in an old afghan, and let the fear soak in, let herself feel everything she'd had to suppress in order to keep functioning during the crisis.

She remembered. She couldn't stop remembering, and knew it would be a long time before the images faded—images of the two people who meant more to her than anything in the world being threatened with a knife. She cried quietly, with the battered exhaustion of a survivor, when she thought of Ricky.

When she thought of Chase, her eyes dried. He was hurt, but he wasn't dead. And he wasn't gone, either. Not yet.

He'd been right, damn him. Even certain heartbreak had seemed safer to her in some perverse way than the uncertainty of risk...and hope was the riskiest feeling of all. It was true that, in an effort to hold something of herself back, she'd never asked him into her bed.

But he'd been wrong, too. She hadn't fallen in love with him because he would leave, and she hadn't made it easy for him to go because secretly that was what she wanted, as well as what she expected, of him.

Pride. Pure, spine-straightening pride was all that had kept her from falling apart and begging him to stay.

Eventually, close to dawn, she dozed off, still huddled up in the afghan on the couch.

The sound of someone at the back door brought her

instantly, thrummingly awake. The moment that first zing of alarm faded, though, she knew. There was no logic to it, but she knew. She wasn't even slightly surprised when she opened the door and saw Chase on her back porch.

He was a mess. Not his clothes—the shirt he wore was a crisp, official-looking khaki. But his hair was dulled from dirt and blood, and beneath his tan he was a pasty gray.

Her mouth went dry with longing, and it took her a minute to speak. ''What are you doing out of the hospital?''

''No need for me to stay,'' he said, ''once they'd stitched me up and pumped me full of antibiotics and a little extra fluid to counter the blood loss.''

''Looks like you talked the deputy right out of the shirt on his back.''

He gave an awkward, one-shoulder shrug and fell silent.

Why wasn't he speaking? Why didn't he smile or hold her or ask her how Ricky was—or how she was, for that matter? ''Do you want to come in and have some coffee, or are you going to go straight to sleep?''

He hesitated. ''I came back to pack,'' he said at last. ''I'm leaving.''

When Chase saw the way the blood drained from Summer's face, he started to reach for her. Involuntarily. Automatically. Pulling his hand back was one of the hardest things he'd ever done.

''Now?'' she said. ''You're leaving *now?*''

Yes, he was leaving her now, when she had no one to fall back on—now, when she badly needed kindness and support and caring. It was a sort of surgery. He'd cut himself out of her life with one quick, brutal stroke.

She would hate him, but she would get over him faster by hating. "It's best this way. I'll have my stuff packed and ready in twenty minutes. If you don't mind if I borrow your truck one more—"

"You can walk away from me, but damned if I'll give you the keys to drive away."

His eyebrows went up at her tone. "I'll call Will or Rosie to come pick me up, then." He turned.

"You don't have permission to use my phone."

He turned back, astonished.

Her eyes were dry. Her chin was up, and those beautiful, full lips were firm...and her face was nearly as white as that nightgown she'd had on last night. "Please don't go, Chase," she said, low, clear, aching. "Please. I love you."

Oh, God. Somehow he made himself turn away and start down the steps, feeling chunks of himself fall away and crumble to dust with every step he took.

The last thing he expected was to have her join him. Walk alongside him. His heart rate went crazy. He thought maybe *he* was going crazy.

"If it was just me," she said conversationally, "I'd put this place up for sale and go with you. Or follow you, and give you more time to come to terms with this. But I can't pull Ricky up by the roots that way."

He didn't speak. He didn't look at her. He just kept putting one foot forward, then the other.

"You've got a real gift with horses," she said. "It's a sin for you to throw that away by living on the road. If you stay here, you can start training. Any fool can see it's what you were meant for. With your rodeo connections it wouldn't take long for you to—"

"For God's sake!" He spun to face her—almost

reaching out to grab her before he stopped himself. "Don't do this to yourself! Don't you have any pride?"

"It doesn't matter!" And she, damn her, reached for him, grabbing his arms—making him hurt with the need to grab her, too, to hold on and hold on—making him wince when she accidentally pulled at the muscle slashed by Wayne's knife.

Summer dropped her hands. "It doesn't matter," she said more quietly. "That's what I finally figured out last night, almost too late, when I saw your blood all over you and Wayne both. Pride means nothing next to what I feel for you. If I thought—if I really believed—that leaving would make you happy, I'd let you go. Or," she said, her voice even lower, "if I believed you didn't love me. Tell me you don't love me, Chase, and I won't say another word."

Out here in the middle of the yard, with the first fresh colors of dawn painting the eastern sky with light and the whole wide world around him, he felt the walls closing in. Tight, suffocating walls. "I can't stay," he rasped. "It doesn't matter if I want to or not. I can't."

"You can." Lightly she touched his arm.

"No!" He pushed her hand away, backing off. "Aren't you listening? What's wrong with you? For God's sake, I almost got your son killed last night! You've got to leave me alone—let me go—"

"You didn't! You saved his life." She came toward him, her hand out, beseeching. "Chase, you aren't blaming yourself for what almost happened, are you? Not when *you're* the reason it didn't happen!"

"I should have done everything differently. I should have figured out about Wayne. I should never—it's just like always." Despair swam up, choking off his breath, blinding him. "Always," he repeated softly. "I just have to be somewhere nearby for the people I care about to get hurt. Or worse.''

''Chase? You don't think you're some kind of jinx, do you?''

He didn't see Summer now. He saw the past and all the highways, all the roads that led nowhere except away. ''It's just the way the world works, Summer. As soon as you start settling in and think something will last, life takes it away. I quit waiting for life to make the first move a long time ago. I learned to keep moving.''

''Tell me,'' she said, and he felt her hand, warm, on his shoulder, ''why did you really leave the rodeo?''

He blinked, her sudden change of subject yanking him back to the present. ''My knee—''

''No.'' She shook her head. ''No, I don't buy that. Sure, it hurts sometimes. But you've been able to do anything you wanted in spite of that, and pain just isn't a good enough reason to make an athlete quit doing what he loves. I think you quit *because* you loved it so much.'' She squeezed his arm once and let go.

His mouth opened, then closed. He had, he discovered, nothing to say. Absolutely nothing. So he did what he'd always done when confronted by something he couldn't face. He turned and left.

Summer's voice floated after him. ''I have to stay close enough to home to hear Ricky if he wakes up,'' she said softly. ''I can't go with you any farther, Chase.''

He just kept walking.

It took Chase thirty minutes to get everything packed. It should have taken about half that, but he couldn't get his mind to stick on anything. He kept stopping and staring off at nothing.

Once he was packed, he realized he couldn't take his duffel with him. It weighed too much for a man on foot, a man with a bad knee and a slashed shoulder, to carry into town. It didn't occur to him to use the phone. It was her phone, not his, and she'd said he didn't have permission.

Will would come get his bag for him. Or Rosie. And if they didn't, what was in that duffel that he couldn't live without? Nothing—not one damned thing, especially when he compared it to what he was walking away from that day.

Still he stood in the small, dreary room off the kennel, looking around with blank eyes for several long minutes. He was forgetting something. His brain wasn't working right, or he'd be able to think of what it was. But it would come to him in a minute. In just a minute…

When he realized what he was looking for—something of hers, anything of hers that he could take away with him—he nearly broke.

He left the deputy's shirt on the bed, set his good hat on top of the duffel near the door and walked out of the kennel wearing his last pair of clean jeans, his hot pink shirt, old cream Stetson and old boots. He had, he realized, finally gotten about as free as a man could be—not even a duffel bag to weigh him down now when he set off down the road.

Nothing but memories.

It was misty outside, but the sun was shining, giving a magical, pearly kind of sheen to everything and dampening Chase's face and hands by the time he reached the gate. Summer's house was about fifty feet south. As he drew near the small frame home he was careful not to look. He couldn't bear to see it, if she was standing there, watching him go.

Yet it wasn't the memories of the woman he was walking out on that haunted him for the first hundred feet down the road as the mist turned into a light drizzle. It wasn't even the old, worn-out memories of the night he'd lost his folks that clung to him, or ghosts from the time that followed, when he lost his aunt to the hospital, then his brother by being placed in foster care. By the time the authorities moved him the first time from one foster home to another, it hadn't mattered. After the second change, he'd liked the moving better than the staying.

No, the memories that blinded him as he left Summer's house behind were from his days on the circuit.

That, he hadn't expected. He hadn't expected to recall the hot shot of adrenaline as he plunged out of the chute on the back of a horse who plumb hated his guts; the sound of the buzzer a split second *after* he parted company with the horse; the laughter, camaraderie and occasional fistfights among friends and acquaintances in the hundred and one honky-tonks he'd passed time in; the sight and sound of the highway beneath his tires as he pointed the hood of his truck at the horizon again.

He'd loved the rodeo. He'd flat-out loved it—for the competition, the horses, the people—and for the chance to be moving on toward something when he headed down the road, not just going away.

There in the middle of the sunny, warm drizzle that was gradually soaking his clothes, revelation struck Chase McGuire square in the heart. He stopped dead.

He *couldn't* avoid what mattered in life. Even when he ran as fast as he could for as long as he could, like he had while he was on the circuit—even when he left so many things behind that he ended up walking down the highway, about as used-up and busted as a man can get—the things that mattered stayed right with him. He couldn't ever leave them behind, no matter how hard he tried.

When he heard the yip-yip-yip behind him, he didn't pay any attention. The noise drew closer, but he ignored it, caught by his revelation. Not until that fool dog's happy yelps sounded right behind him did he turn and look.

Kelpie raced up the road at him. When she got there she spun around and did her happy dance, the tight-circling silliness she used to greet people she loved. He gaped at her, trying to figure out how the hell she'd gotten out. He was certain he'd latched the gate when he left. Maybe he'd been distracted, but that action was too automatic for anyone raised on a ranch to omit.

Slowly, disbelievingly, his gaze lifted. A hundred feet back down the road, a woman in old jeans, a faded flannel shirt and wildly tangled whiskey-colored hair was closing the big gate. The one she'd obviously opened in order to let her dog go racing off down the highway after him.

She looked at him for a second. He couldn't have said, from that distance, what her expression was. Then she turned around and walked back to her house.

Summer honestly believed she wasn't crying as she climbed the steps to her back porch. Not really crying. Sniffing a bit, maybe, but that hardly counted. She was too tired to cry over that damned stubborn cowboy she'd fallen in love with.

The one it looked like she wasn't ever going to see again.

By the time she was back in her kitchen, she was "not crying" so hard that she didn't hear so much as a footfall to warn her.

When his hand landed on her shoulder, she jumped nearly out of her skin. "I brought your dog back," he said softly.

She didn't turn. He might not have agreed with her about whether she'd really been crying or not if he saw her face. She didn't speak, either, because she wasn't at all able to.

"That was a stupid, manipulative thing to do, sending your dog after me. What in the hell were you thinking of?"

Somehow, his anger made her smile. But he couldn't see that, because she still didn't turn around. "Maybe I wanted to make you come back, just to prove I could."

"Yeah," he said. "When I first saw her tearing up the road at me, I wondered if that was it, but I decided it wasn't. I thought maybe…it was because you didn't want me to be alone, even if I was the stupid jerk who was hurting you. I thought you might somehow know that I was breaking apart under all that loneliness, but didn't know how to stop, even though I love you so much it's been killing me. I thought—"

She turned and flung herself into his arms—his arms that were open and ready for her, that wrapped around her so tightly she knew it had to hurt one or both of them, but she didn't care.

"I thought," he said, his voice muffled, his words fractured by the kisses he pressed into her hair, her cheek, her throat, "that I wasn't ever going to be rid of you, not if I had your dog with me—and you weren't going to let me leave without something of you traveling with me, were you? So I thought I might just as well come back." He paused, pressing his cheek against hers. "That's when I got so happy I could hardly stand myself."

She felt his happiness—in the way his cheek bunched with his smile, in the pounding of his heart—or maybe that was her heart racing like a horse at full gallop. "I didn't think you were coming back."

"I missed you," he said. "I was a hundred feet away from your house and I missed you so much I almost started bawling when I saw your dog headed for me, and I knew it just wasn't any use. I can't leave." He shook his head, marveling. "All this time, I thought the staying was the part that was so hard, the part I couldn't handle. Turned out I had it exactly backward."

"Stubborn man," she agreed, and grabbed his head, pulled it to her and kissed him.

Eventually, when they each had their breath back, or most of it, and their tongues were pretty much back in their usual places, too, she asked what any woman would ask then. "When did you know you loved me? And why didn't you *say* something?"

He smiled that slow, wicked smile of his. "About ten minutes ago," he said, "when I saw your dog come running up that highway. And I told you as soon as—ouch! You shouldn't go pinching a wounded man." He rubbed his side, smiling down at her, his life-filled eyes glowing. "I didn't say that's when I fell in love," he added softly. "That probably happened about the time you opened your door to me that first day, and I discovered I'd been waiting all my life to meet a lady with skinny hips, summer-sky eyes and so much love it just spills over onto all your strays.''

Summer answered promptly, without saying a word. Chase gave her reply his full attention, sinking his hand into the thickness of her hair and his tongue into the sweetness of her mouth. Taking his time—because he had time. For once in his life, he had the time to savor, because he wasn't going to be leaving. Not anytime soon. Not at all…provided he got the right answer to his next question.

He caught one of her busy hands when it started to make a trip to his belt buckle. He meant to chuckle, but it came out more like a groan. "Easy there. I'm not feeling much in control here.''

Her trapped fingers wiggled, tickling his middle. "I want to show you my bedroom,'' she whispered.

Oh, lordy, he did want to see it, too. But Chase McGuire, a man who'd risked his life regularly from the age of fifteen on, was having one hell of a time getting together the courage to say what he needed to say. "Hold on a minute,'' he told her, and set her from him—not far, just far enough so he could look at her when he said the next part.

Only the next part, it seemed, wouldn't get said. The closest he could come was, "Do you think Maudie would mind giving the groom away?''

Her breath caught. "Chase, I want to make sure I've got this clear. Are you proposing to me? Proposing *marriage?*''

He nodded, more frightened than he'd been the first time he'd lowered himself on the back of a ton of pure, ornery bull.

"That's a pretty lousy proposal, you know.''

He nodded again.

"Yes."

He waited.

Summer's mouth twitched. "That's my answer to your proposal, Chase. *Yes.*"

"Thank God." His arms went around her—the good one and the injured one, and if he was dizzy, no doubt it was the earlier blood loss just now catching up with him. "Thank God," he said again, grinning like a fool but feeling sure, for the first time in a long time, that he wasn't being one.

And for several long moments Chase McGuire stood there in that small, cozy kitchen in the house that was going to be his first home in twenty-three years, holding the woman he loved, swaying slightly back and forth, smiling and smiling out the kitchen window.

It was still drizzling outside, and the sun was still shining. So it wasn't surprising that through that window he saw the gentle colors of a rainbow forming somewhere near the horizon. It was a lovely thing, that rainbow. But he wouldn't be chasing any more of those phantoms of air and damp, dust and light. Because Chase McGuire had found his own rainbow's end at last.

*   *   *   *   *

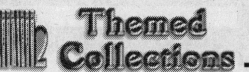

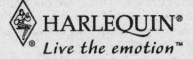

Harlequin Historicals®
Historical Romantic Adventure!

From rugged lawmen and valiant knights to defiant heiresses and spirited frontierswomen, Harlequin Historicals will capture your imagination with their dramatic scope, passion and adventure.

Harlequin Historicals . . . they're too good to miss!

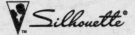

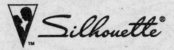

SILHOUETTE *Romance*

From first love to forever, these love stories
are fairy tale romances for today's woman.

Silhouette
Desire

Modern, passionate reads that are powerful and provocative.

Silhouette
SPECIAL EDITION™

Emotional, compelling stories that capture the intensity
of living, loving and creating a family in today's world.

Silhouette
INTIMATE MOMENTS™

A roller-coaster read that delivers romantic thrills
in a world of suspense, adventure and more.